Cupán Fae Presents

FIERCE

A Hopepunk Anthology

Cameron Armstrong
Paul Carroll
Quinn Clancy
Kat Dodd
Axel Kelly

ISBN: 9798486306839

Table of Contents

INTRODUCTION

When the world began to turn to hell, there were hopes it wouldn't last very long. A few weeks. A few months. As I write this, we're a year and half into a global pandemic, and we've survived on the hope that things would return to normal.

Hopepunk is all about the fight, keeping it up no matter the odds because the alternative is giving up. When Cupán Fae lost its regular meet-ups in a coffee shop in Dublin, we turned to the Internet to keep us connected. When our home-away-from-home, Octocon, went online, we followed. Communities gathered to the safest spaces they could, and while it hasn't always been ideal, it's been our way of fighting the dread of whatever fresh disasters would rear their ugly heads.

I wouldn't have made it through the pandemic without the company of my friends in Cupán Fae. They have always been stalwart companions, a family found between pages and word counts and hot chocolates even on a hot summer's evening.

In the pages of this book, there are stories of survival, of friendship, of love. There are battles against systems that would keep us down, and struggles to keep on keeping on. Regular readers of Cupán Fae's anthologies will recognise the familiar names to follow, with a friendly new face to add to the mix.

And maybe that's the beauty of keeping hopeful, no matter the state of the world. It allowed us to greet new people, to make new friends, and to keep telling stories.

The fight, and the hope, are worth it.

Is mise le meas,

Paul Carroll

September 2021

SLEEP OR SWIM – CAMERON ARMSTRONG

The alarms sounded just as the druidess was preparing to dive into the lake. Red lights flashed in the sky and sirens belted out a shrill warning from somewhere beyond the clouds. The druidess grimaced, contemplating whether to ignore it – at least long enough to jump in and feel the icy bite against her skin – but thought the better of it and retreated from the precipice. Roberta would not be pleased if she was late to take up her post. The druidess cast a forlorn glance around the rocks, the forest, the crystalline water, then reached a hand up to her eyes and pried away an invisible blindfold.

The bare metallic walls of the ship's interior flashed into view. Kelly had to blink a few times to adjust to the glare of the fluorescent lights. Her ears thrummed with the guttural vibrations of the engine, buried somewhere below her feet under layers of plasteel armastructure and hyperfiber cables. She peeled the visigoggles from her face and straightened her back. Shame none of that in-world exercise transferred over to her real joints and muscles. Her limbs had gone stiff after sitting inert for so long, so she took a moment to shake herself loose. Then she set the visigoggles on the mantle beside the hoverchair, triggering the immersion chamber's sliding door.

Kelly tugged impatiently at her hair as she tied it back into a slipshod ponytail. She'd come closer to bona fide swimming than ever before, this time. It thrilled her as much as terrified her. She'd given up trying to wade in from the shore; it was unnerving to see the water level slowly increase, consuming her ankles, then her knees, then her waist. Throwing herself in was her new strategy, one she was almost sure was going to work. It wasn't like she would drown if it went badly – the simulation would shut down before any mortal harm befell her. Of course, just when she'd worked up the nerve to jump, Roberta had to interrupt her. She would have to conquer her fear all over again when her next break came.

She had to duck her head as she made her way down the catwalk toward the mess hall, dodging steam expulsions and shorting electric circuits. There were burn marks all along the corridor from the fire they'd had a month ago. They'd nearly lost the whole C-Deck that day. What would that have left them with? The maintenance wing and the freezer. She clucked her tongue as she hefted herself up the narrow ladder and up to the main deck. Would've hardly been worth salvaging if that's all that was left.

Roberta was waiting by the monitoring station they'd rigged up across from the food processor. They hadn't had much choice about where to set up their base of operations – the galley was the largest area that hadn't been contaminated besides the maintenance wing, and it was far more comfortable. Couches and a few tables lined one side of the room, the other the cooking area. Not that either of them had used the stove or anything else besides the processor. Danny had been the chef, and his brains were splattered across the observation deck window. She sighed as she sat down in one of the swivel chairs across from Roberta. Danny had been cute. Maybe there could have been something there. Maybe he would have made her spicy jambalaya, if she's asked. He was always going on about the virtues of fresh ingredients over synthetic. Would soil-grown chili peppers still have the same kick? She'd never find out – the hydroponics lab had been the first to be overrun.

"What's the latest? Any movement?" she asked the back of Roberta's head.

"Nothing to worry about. Did you have a nice swim?"

"Didn't get a chance, actually."

"Hm. Waste of time anyway."

"Is it? Excuse me for trying to learn something new. I'm challenging myself, Roberta. Trying to keep my mind occupied. So what if I can't use it outside the simulation?"

"I mean that – that's the waste of time. Simulations. You want to learn to swim, you need lessons. Practical ones."

"Yeah, well, are you gonna teach me?"

"I'm a little busy keeping this wreck afloat, as it happens."

Kelly gave a stiff nod. "Right. So, if there's nothing to worry about, why'd you flip the emergency switch instead of just knocking on the door?"

"You know what time it is, don't you?"

"Uh–"

Kelly flung her eyes about the room for a clue. She felt an icy stab of guilt as she glimpsed Walton's novelty cat-clock hanging above the water recycler.

"Oh, damn. Sorry. Guess I was really in the zone."

Kelly chewed aimlessly on the end of her ponytail until Roberta turned herself around from the monitors. The woman's face was creased in a deep-set frown, as always. Her head appeared freshly shaved. Her arm muscles rippled as she leaned forward, folding her hands together and resting her elbows on her knees.

"Kelly," she said. "We need to talk."

"You sure now's a good time?" Kelly motioned to the grainy image on the rightmost screen. "That Sludge pile looks like it's on the move."

Roberta didn't flinch. "It's not a problem. You being late is."

Kelly nodded, but the shifting image on the display distracted her. The Sludge pile – a particularly large one – was oozing its way along the transport bay ceiling, pushing wiry tendrils ahead of itself as it probed its way around loose tubing and pipework. Kelly could trace its path easily enough. It was encroaching on a ventilation duct. The fan blades were still spinning, but the Sludge wouldn't mind having a few of its tendrils sliced off – it would gum up the machinery and then slide through the gaps like gelatin pressing itself through a meat grinder. They'd seen the same thing happen all over the ship.

"Do you have an explanation?" Roberta said.

"Uh, yeah. Sure. That simulation Jefferson programmed – you know, 'Ancient Island' or whatever he called it. It's amazing. Like he made it from memory, or something. There's this lake – the water's so clear, it reflects the sky like a mirror. It feels like you're swimming in the sky. And – it's the weirdest thing – it's so quiet there. It's only ever *you*. Alone. Total isolation. It sounds awful, I know, but when you're there, walking in the woods, climbing the rocks, it's so peaceful. Makes you lose track of time. Makes you feel like time doesn't exist, even. It's crazy."

Through all of this, Roberta kept staring at her, stonelike, while the Sludge inched closer to the duct. Kelly had been tracking it as she talked, waiting for Roberta to do something, and now she pointed a finger at the screen.

"Roberta, seriously, it's almost at the vent."

"I said it's not a problem."

Before Kelly could respond, the Sludge pile reached the duct. It stretched out several probing fronds toward the fan blades. Kelly was about to give a cry of alarm when a fiery blast consumed the screen, then disappeared a second later. She caught a glimpse of the Sludge in the corner of the screen, creeping its way back across the pipes as fast as its mess of appendages would allow.

"The hell was that?" Kelly said, leaning across the table. The incinerated Sludge lost its grip, dropped from the ceiling and banged off the hull of one of the abandoned all-terrain vehicles left in the bay.

"A booby-trap I rigged up."

"Oh. Is that what you were doing on your shift?"

"Didn't take that long. Only needed to open up some gas valves, build a little device capable of producing a spark. I placed them around some of the critical junctions." She pointed behind her own head, where a boxy device was affixed over the galley doorway. Kelly could see a few others on the monitors screens – the engineering level, the hydraulics system chamber, the maintenance deck. "Once the Sludge trips the sensor, boom."

"Ring the doorbell, get blasted by a fireball," Kelly said. "Nice. Where'd the explosives come from?"

"No explosives. Just rerouted a couple of the fuel channels."

"Wait, fuel channels? You're siphoning fuel for this?"

Roberta shrugged. "So what? We're not using the superdrive for much else."

"What about if we need to set a new course?"

"This is dead space. New course to where? Deader space?"

"We don't know what's out there, that's the point. Rogue planets. Flyby comets. Search parties!"

"How about another asteroid carrying a hostile alien lifeform?"

Kelly ignored her cynicism. "If the scanners pick up an outpost or a hospitable world within jump distance, it's not like we can just drift there. Might be lightyears away. Don't you think we're better off conserving fuel for when we need it?" She gestured to the screen. "I mean, flaming booby-traps are cool and all, but we've been getting by fine with just zapping the Sludge when it gets too close."

Instead of answering, Roberta bowed her head and rubbed her eye sockets with her thumbs.

"See, Kelly, this is why we need to talk," she said without looking up. "There isn't going to be any hospitable planet. No friendly little outpost to take us in."

"You can't know that for sure. We've been broadcasting our distress beacon for months now. You know how far radio waves travel in that amount of time?" Roberta lifted a weary eye. "Okay, I don't either, but it's pretty damn far. Wayne told me that much."

"Wayne's dead, Kelly."

"I mean, he could just be in some kind of coma–"

"He's shambling around the engineering level with Sludge coming out his eyes. He's dead, alright? For all intents and purposes. And we're gonna be next. That is, unless we…"

Abruptly, Roberta stood and paced across the galley. Kelly tracked her movement, a tiny tremor of dread shooting down her spine.

"Unless we what?"

Roberta turned to face her. Her expression seemed carved from granite.

"Freeze ourselves."

A nervous grin spread across Kelly's face.

"Right. When there's a crisis, just hop in the freezer and sleep it out. Is that what they're teaching kids now instead of Stop, Drop and Roll?"

Roberta kept staring at her. Kelly found herself losing control of her tongue, speaking faster and faster.

"Come on, what would that accomplish? If we put ourselves in the freezer for even a single afternoon the whole ship will be overrun. Those flaming-doorbell things you rigged up won't keep the Sludge out forever. I mean, how many possible breach points are there? Air vents, trash chutes, toilet plumbing."

"No, they won't keep them out forever," Roberta said. "Even if they could, we'd run out of fuel. I calculate it'll take about sixteen years for the tanks to fully deplete, assuming the Sludge piles keep coming at the rate we've been seeing. But cosmic radiation would have fried the freezer's electronic subsystems long before then."

"Uh – right. So, it's a bad idea. Why'd you even bring it up?"

"The freezers are a closed system, for one. They run on their own internal power sources. And they're airtight. Out here, with half the ship smashed up, they're the only Sludge-proof environment we have."

Kelly blinked in disbelief. She gave a violent shake of her head, as if that might cause Roberta's words to tumble out her ears and shatter on the floor.

"Roberta, you can't be serious. You want to just lock ourselves in and go to sleep? Let the Sludge take over the rest of the ship?"

The muscular woman strode over to the galley's viewport and leaned against the glass.

"It's going to take over it eventually, one way or another. This way, we can make sure it doesn't take over *us*."

Kelly made no effort to hide her horror. Roberta's proposal was tantamount to suicide. It had been a hard few months ever since the outbreak, definitely, but they were getting by. Even if the other members of the crew were gone, the two of them had found ways to survive on their own. She couldn't fathom why Roberta would want to just give up. Going into cryo-sleep in these conditions would mean going to sleep for good. Not to mention that if – *when* – they were discovered by some passerby, be they scavengers, pirates or friendly patrols, their life signals would be impossible to detect. Whoever stumbled across the ship would determine it to be overrun with an alien contagion and either blast it out of the sky or abandon it wholesale, missing altogether that there were still two human-flavored Popsicles on board.

"Roberta," Kelly said slowly, rising from her seat at the table, "we can't just give up like that. I mean, I know it's been tough, but – we're still here. You and me. We can get through this, still."

"Are we both still here, though?"

"Huh?"

Roberta turned from the viewport. The view outside was starless, void. Kelly had a hard time looking at it – it seemed like the yawning blackness of space was pushing its way through the window, like molasses squeezing through a pinhole. She wondered how it didn't make Roberta queasy.

"Are you still here, Kelly?" Roberta said.

Kelly tapped her chest and sides. "Think so."

"Don't be an idiot. You know what I mean."

Kelly stared at her blankly.

"The immersion chamber! Whenever you're not on watch duty you're in there, losing yourself. You spend just as much time in virtual sims as you do here on this ship – more, sometimes, since you were late taking over this shift. I let you stay plugged in this time, just to see when you'd make it back. You know how long you were in there? Four hours straight! Four hours of climbing trees and chasing wild goats, or whatever the hell it is you do in there. That's not healthy, Kelly."

Kelly tried her best to hold back a laugh, but one sputtered out anyway.

"Holy hell, Roberta – I'm sorry I was late and all, but you're not my mom. I thought we got over all that video-games-melt-your-brain B.S. centuries ago."

"You're not listening, Kelly."

"Because you're talking crazy! Look, I get that you busted your ass setting up those firebomb things, but I think you need to take it down a few notches. I mean, are you hearing yourself? Hop in the freezer, like that'll fix everything? Really? Maybe you should try Ancient Island yourself – you need help taking the edge off after these long shifts."

Roberta's fist crashed on the surface of the galley table, startling Kelly to silence.

"Would you take this seriously? For once? These are life and death decisions here. No more quips. No more inane little smiles. Like that one. Wipe it off, damn it – I mean it!"

Kelly did so. Roberta's breathing became slow and methodical as she tried to collect herself. She lifted her fist from the table and crossed her arms, then turned back to the window.

"So, what are you saying?" Kelly asked. "You don't want me going in the chamber anymore? There's less drastic ways to fix this, you know. I could just set a timer, or–"

"Enough, Kelly," said Roberta. "Just tell me. Do you agree, or no?"

"Agree with what? The thing about chasing goats? It was plenty healthy. Basically the most cathartic moment of my life, after spending weeks cramped up in here."

"No, damn it. Will you agree to…"

Roberta didn't finish the thought. Her eyes met Kelly's, and the answer was clear. She clenched her jaw and held up a hand as if in surrender, then marched past her on her way out to the crew's quarters.

"You're gonna get us both killed," she muttered from the doorway.

"Aw, Roberta. Come on, stay. Let's work this out. We're a team. We need each other."

"Exactly – we need each other. I'd freeze myself, if I could. Get out of this hell. But then you'd be left here alone, and you can't fend them off by yourself."

Roberta gestured to the screen. As Kelly turned her head, she saw a swarm of Sludge piles converging on the same air vent as before.

"So I'm stuck here, waiting for you to wake up," she continued. "Only, I'm starting to doubt that's ever going to happen."

Without another word, she disappeared through the portal. The sliding doors hissed closed behind her, leaving a bemused Kelly standing in the middle of the galley, staring at the images of Sludge piles jostling each other for the position closest to the vent. The winner of the little tussle was promptly fireblasted. Its gelatinous body dropped from the ceiling in a fleshy heap. The survivors slid back and pondered their next move.

Kelly grumbled to herself as she moved toward the monitoring station. Roberta was the one who needed to wake up – literally, if she thought sleeping in the freezer chambers was going to fix their problems. The two of them were shipwreck survivors stranded on a desert island; if they wanted to live, they needed to work with what they had – lash some trees together, build a shelter, hunt wild boar, not curl up and take a nap.

Kelly scratched her forehead and squinted at the buzzing screens. Maybe the island metaphor didn't quite work, considering they were trapped on their own ship, not an uncharted planet. Survivors on a life raft, then. What they needed was a rescue – that was it. Kelly glanced at the console displaying their radio broadcast frequencies. No hits yet. But if they held out long enough, drifted far enough, something was bound to bounce back. It was only a matter of time.

She nodded to herself as she cycled through the different cameras, scanning the various decks of the ship for Sludge. The piles in the vehicle bay were sulking in the corner of the room, reluctant to make another pass at the vent. Good, then – she could focus on the communications tower, where two rather large piles were squeezing their way under the emergency lock. After the collision some of the hydraulics had been damaged, meaning not all the automatic failsafes had engaged properly. Almost thirty percent of the ship had been exposed to the vacuum of space, sucking out a large portion of their recyclable oxygen along with Langford. The corridor joining B-Deck to the tower's base was one of these breaches. How the Sludge was able to survive in a heatless, airless environment was beyond her, but she wasn't a biologist. Langford was – or had been, anyway.

Kelly straightened up and moved to the ladder leading to the deck below. It was only a short walk to the airlock from there. On a rack outside of the hatch hung her spacesuit, looking somewhat worn after so many impromptu repair missions. It was singed with spark burns from her laser-welder, which now rested in a holster at the hip. She checked the battery before suiting up. There was more than enough juice to zap some slime, but she made a note to change it anyway once she got back. Some of the radiation shielding on the hull had been knocked loose in the collision and would need to be welded into place if they ever wanted to get back onto the bridge without being fried by gamma rays.

Thinking of the abandoned bridge reminded her: Julia still had that box of tampons she'd borrowed before the crash. Kelly never had the chance to ask for them back before the Sludge's native asteroid punched a hole through the cockpit and killed everyone inside. The box had to be on Julia's reanimated corpse, shuffling around somewhere near the pilot's console. Damn whoever had programmed the ship's fabricator and forgot to include a category for feminine hygiene products. Hadn't that been the internal systems operator's job – whatwashisname, Peter? Patrick? Typical man.

On second thought, Julia might have passed the box on to Roberta before the impact. Kelly considered the possibility as she stepped through the airlock, wrinkling her nose as the strange sensation of weightlessness settled in her gut. Roberta was the only other woman on the crew, and if Julia had forgotten to stock up after their rest stop at Kappa-Station, there was every possibility that Roberta had, too.

Jefferson had said something about transition surgery, though – not that he was the most reliable source for gossip, considering he'd all the spacegrass he smoked. But wasn't Roberta taking hormone injections, or something? Kelly had overheard Stevie mention it to the boys over lunch one time, but she didn't know. It wasn't like she could ask. She'd seen the woman knock the sparring robot in the exercise hall flat with a single punch. Then again, considering Roberta had just invited her to participate in what amounted to a suicide pact, maybe nothing was off-limits anymore.

As Kelly secured her tether and pushed herself out into space, she made up her mind to rifle through Roberta's drawers the next time she was out on a shift. She might dig up a clue as to why she had suddenly come up with the idea of freezing themselves. She knew Roberta liked reading – if she found copies of *20,000 Leagues* or *Under the Sea* or *Lord of the Flies* on her nightstand it would be a clear sign that she was heading into a downward spiral.

It didn't take long for Kelly to reach the B-Deck corridor's airlock. The jet propulsion system in her spacesuit made it easy to maneuver her way around the outside of the ship. She keyed open the hatch, disconnected her tether and slipped into the compression chamber. She kept her helmet on even as the room was pumped full of oxygen – as soon as she opened the airlock door to re-enter the ship it would all escape again. There was also the risk that some Sludge was hiding in a crevice overhead, ready to drop on unsuspecting passersby. They'd warned Jefferson not to travel around the unsecured parts of the ship unprotected. He'd said it made him too sweaty, and besides, the flamethrowers he'd retrofitted from the heavy diggers would keep them at bay. Now his pores seeped alien muck instead.

The gravity panels in this section of the ship still had some charge, so Kelly was able to walk around with a semblance of normalcy. She pulled out her laser-cutter and made her way to the emergency seal. A few tendrils were squeezing through the gap already. She flicked the switch on the cutter and was about to start slicing – bracing herself for the stinking discharge that spurted out whenever the thin membrane that served as the Sludge's 'skin' was penetrated – when she noticed that the tendrils were tinged blue. Not only that, they were changing colour in a clear pattern: blue, then mottled grey, then blue again.

It took Kelly a moment to understand what she was seeing. Sludge was translucent, meaning it wasn't really changing its colour; instead, light from the other side of the emergency lock was passing through its body. A flashing light, specifically. The realization made her hesitate. Then she was cutting through the tendrils, spilling oily puss on the grav-pads, and hastily re-wiring the door control panel. After a few false starts she found the correct sequence and the emergency lock sprang open. She gave no thought to how she might close it again – her mind was fixed on reaching the blue light. It was there, flickering from a console in the middle of the communications control center. Her heart leapt in her chest as she moved across the room to it, kicking the punctured Sludge piles out of her way and spraying the walls with bile.

Her heartbeat accelerated as she reached the console. The light did belong to the transponder after all. Seeing its steady blink was like seeing a lighthouse flash in the middle of a storm; it was an undeniable confirmation that salvation was at hand. Someone had received their distress call and was trying to get into contact.

Kelly was so overwhelmed that she stood stiff in front of the console for a full thirty seconds. Then she flew into action, flipping switches and twisting dials to try and bring the signal into focus, patching it through the comm link in her helmet. Briefly she thought she could make out the sound of a voice – a human voice – buried somewhere beneath the garbled static. She hit playback again and again, trying to isolate the voice, but it was lost in the noise. She frowned and pored over the data readouts, doing her best to grasp why, though the frequencies seemed to be in alignment, nothing intelligible was coming through. She pulled the microphone close and was about to record a message of her own before seeing that its wires had been shredded. She threw the tangled mess against the console in frustration.

At that moment, something rubbery landed on her shoulder. It knocked her forward, doubling her over the console. She spun around, reeling from shock, expecting to see a gushing ball of slime rising to swallow her whole. Instead, she saw a face.

It was Stevie. The glass in his helmet was broken, so the skin of his face had become petrified in the extreme cold of open space. Congealed sludge streamed from his nostrils, mouth and eye sockets.

He staggered towards her like a stiff plastic toy, arms outstretched, legs bent at crooked angles. Kelly gave a shriek and dove over the console. She grabbed a loose chair and tossed it against the console's base. It didn't slow him down for long – somehow the Sludge controlling his corpse had enough control of his motor functions to make him clamber over the obstruction after her. Kelly tried to run back to where she'd entered the communications tower, but more Sludge piles appeared, as if sensing her peril. She brandished the laser cutter and sliced at the closest few. They fell back, writhing like dissected worms, but more converged to replace them.

Growing desperate, Kelly looked about the room for anything that could help her escape – a fire extinguisher, a rope, a hatchet. Everything in the tower was dark save for the blinking light of the transponder. She could barely see three feet in front of her, which made fending off the clustering Sludge piles nearly impossible. And Stevie's corpse was still coming after her, no matter what she threw at it. He made a swipe at her and succeeded in hooking his hand around the laser-cutter holster. She managed to pull the cutter free before twisting away, the holster tearing loose from her suit as she did so.

Before long she realized she'd backed herself into a corner. The door behind her was sealed shut – *of course* this one's emergency lock actually worked. There was no opening it from this side. She faced the swarm and contemplated cutting a hole through her own helmet with the laser. Would having all the air sucked from her lungs and her eyeballs flash-frozen be more or less painful than being squeezed and gnawed to death by a horde of ooze-monsters?

The laser-cutter – that was it! Kelly kicked over a table to knock Stevie back a few more steps, then fired up the tool and began slicing the floor. It was a rough job, but all she needed was a hole wide enough to dive through. Beneath the grav-plate flooring there were wires and support beams and insulation. She dialled the cutter up to its maximum setting and seared the grav-plates loose from their joints. The plasma beam ripped through every obstacle in seconds. Soon she felt the chunk of metal go loose, although with the layers of plastic and wiring beneath it . She slammed her foot down onto it and it broke away, sailing out into space. It left behind a gap just large enough for her to scramble through. Stevie made a leap across the room for her leg, but she batted him away with the butt of the cutter and jettisoned out into open space.

And here she'd thought Stevie had been a creep while he was still alive. He'd always been a bit more hands-on than she'd felt comfortable with, but this was on another level.

A few Sludge piles crowded at the edge of the hole, then started pushing their way after her. But it didn't matter – out here she had superior mobility. She activated the jets in her suit and banked to starboard, flying past the outside of the communications tower window. Her breath ran hot against the glass and fogged up her faceplate. She flew far enough from the breach to feel safe, then patched in to the ship's comm system and tried to hail Roberta. As she lifted her finger to press the call button on the side of her helmet, she realized the laser-cutter was still in her hand. There was no holster to put it in anymore, so she took out the battery, folded it up, then slipped both components into one of the utility pockets on the arm of her suit.

Excitement started to trickle back in as she waited for Roberta to pick up. Someone had heard their distress call! Someone knew they were out here. It was only a matter of time before they were found. Sure, they would need to find a way to establish contact with their would-be rescuers, though she didn't know exactly how they'd go about doing that. The best way to do that would be to isolate the frequency and send a message of their own, but all the equipment they needed to do that was in the tower. She didn't relish the idea of going back in there anytime soon.

As she tried to come up with an alternative, Roberta finally picked up the other end of the line.

"Kelly? What is it?"

"Oh my god, Roberta! You won't believe what happened!"

"You found that box you were looking for."

"Huh? No. Wait, do you know where they are?"

"Didn't you lend it to Julia?"

"Yes. How'd you–? Never mind. Listen, I was just in the comm tower to clear out some Sludge when I saw the transponder light flashing. Someone picked up our distress beacon and sent a ping back!"

Silence on the other end.

"Roberta?"

"They sent a ping back?"

"Yeah, like a 'we read you' kind of message."

"There was no audio?"

"Uh – no. I mean, I don't think so. I didn't exactly get a ton of time to look into it. The place was crawling with Sludge, remember? Plus, Stevie was in there." Kelly shuddered. "He hasn't changed much, really."

"Hang on."

Kelly floated alongside the ship as she waited. She made a point to keep her eyes fixed on a static object – in this case, the radio antennae protruding from the top of the communications tower. It still daunted her, looking out in the vastness of deep space – the incalculable distances, the unfathomable immensity. People often compared spacewalking to swimming in an ocean. But she knew that was an unfair comparison – one meant to steel the cosmonaut's wits against what they intrinsically knew to be true: if they were to cut their tether and push off into the black, they would travel forever – an *eternity* – through a boundless void, and would likely never encounter another person or object until time itself collapsed upon them. To look out at the stars from deep space was to stare into the face of infinity; and for a finite being such as herself, its face was terrifying.

"Kelly, are you there?" crackled Roberta's voice.

"Yeah, I'm here. What were you doing?"

"I'm just sitting down at the monitoring station now. You called while I was working out."

"Oh. Sorry."

"It's not important. Kelly, are you sure you saw the transponder light blinking?"

"Sure I'm sure. I nearly died because of it."

"Well, that's not what I'm seeing on the screens."

"The place was crawling with Sludge. They're probably just blocking your view."

"No. They all went after you through that hole you cut in the hull. Check the starboard side of the B-Deck access corridor."

Kelly felt the blood in her veins freeze solid. She piloted her suit in the direction Roberta had indicated. After a moment she spotted some dark blobs squelching their way along the exterior of the ship. They seemed to be moving toward her, even though she was drifting several meters from the ship itself.

"What about Stevie?" she asked, her throat suddenly feeling very dry.

"Went with them. Only, he wasn't wearing a suit, so he just tumbled off into space."

Kelly gulped. If there was anything still left of him – if the Sludge was somehow able to keep his brain alive, even in that state – he'd be staring into the same abyss as she was until every last star in the universe had collapsed, dispelled its heat and ceased to shine.

"You've gotta be missing something," Kelly said into the comm-link. "It was there – flashing. I saw it with my own eyes."

"There's no light coming from the console besides some sparks from shorted circuits."

"So what are you telling me?" Kelly rasped. "I'm making it all up?"

"I don't know. Are you?"

"No! Check diagnostics. Maybe there's been a power outage. The place was really smashed up – maybe the conduits to the generator are damaged."

Roberta was silent for a few maddening seconds.

"A couple of the conduits are offline, sure, but there's still two feeding it power." She paused. "The link may have gone dead."

"Why would that happen? Someone was trying to make contact. I know it!"

"It could have been radio emissions from a neutron star scrambling up the sensors. A pulsar could do the same thing."

Kelly grimaced. "It wasn't a damn pulsar, Roberta. I heard a voice."

"A voice."

"Yes, a voice! In the static. It sounded like someone was on the other side, trying to hail us."

There was a bitter sigh on the other end of the line.

"A voice, Kelly? Really? Do you realize how convenient that sounds?"

"Convenient? What about this is convenient? I almost got mauled by Sludge trying to match the frequencies!"

"Convenient because a few hours after I suggest we freeze ourselves, suddenly you've discovered a magical radio beacon that I can't find any trace of. Not only that, but it's got a 'voice', which somehow proves that we're about to be rescued."

"Doesn't it?"

"Just see for yourself."

A holographic image flashed in the corner of Kelly's view, generated by her helmet's internal projector. The image showed the interior of the communications tower. Roberta had patched her through to the same camera that they were using to surveil the room from their monitoring station in the galley. The camera panned left to right, revealing heaps of furniture and equipment strewn across the floor as Kelly had made her escape, as well as the hole she'd cut. Through it's night-vision lens she could tell that there were no Sludge piles left, nor was there any sign of Stevie. The camera zoomed in on the console in the center of the room. No blue light blinked. There didn't seem to be any electricity running to the console at all – the entire array had gone dark.

"That can't be right," Kelly said as the image vanished. "I know what I saw."

"And I know what I saw. Nothing."

"Roberta, something's wrong. There was a message. I didn't just see it, I heard it. You have to believe me."

Roberta didn't answer for a long time.

"Just come back to the ship, Kelly. I'll relieve you early."

"Relieve me? My shift's only just started."

"I know. And obviously you're not thinking straight. That whole thing with the Sludge – and what happened with Stevie. You need to rest."

"Not thinking straight? I'm not crazy, Roberta – there was a light on the console!"

Kelly cringed at the shrillness of her own voice. She certainly didn't sound like a reasonable, level-headed, un-crazy person. She took in a breath and was about to try another tack when Roberta came through again.

"Maybe you're right."

"I – what?"

"About the electricity. Maybe something's wrong with the conduits."

Kelly was too surprised to think of a response. Roberta went on: "Come back on board. You rest, I'll take the rest of your shift. Try to work out if something's interfering with the power flow."

"Uh, yeah. Okay."

"Out."

The other end of the line clicked, and Kelly was alone again. She frowned to herself, unsure of how to feel. Pissed off because Roberta had insinuated that she was either lying or imagining things? Relieved because she had apparently changed her mind? Relief was the nicer feeling of the two. She decided to settle on that one, pushing her indignation from her mind. Roberta was just on edge. She was too, after the debacle with Stevie and the Sludge. If she was honest, the thought of ending her shift early seemed heavenly. Ten more hours of patrols, odd maintenance jobs, garbage duty and twiddling her thumbs while she tracked Sludge piles across the screens did not sound appealing. Her nerves were frayed enough as it was – she didn't want to have to sit around wondering when the next attack would come.

As Kelly reached the crew's quarters airlock and passed through the hatch, the fatigue she'd been ignoring up to now caught up with her. She didn't bother with hanging up the spacesuit on the rack as she re-entered the controlled atmosphere of the ship's interior. Prying herself out of it seemed like it would take an even greater effort than simply walking back to the galley with it on. She only removed the helmet so she could scratch at her itchy face and peel the sweaty strands of hair away from her forehead.

It wasn't just the scare with Stevie that was hanging over her. By the time she'd reached the portal to the galley, a profound sense of anticipation had overcome her. The discovery at the tower was a tremendous thing. The light had been flashing. Someone had been calling. Rescue, after all this time, was within reach. She didn't know how she could possibly sleep with that knowledge burning in her mind.

Well, there was a simple solution to that, she thought. A return to the Ancient Island would clear her head. She always felt rejuvenated after a good immersion session. She'd never been a spiritual person, but she'd spent enough time among simulated trees, hills and fields to make her wonder if the Neo-naturalists hadn't been on to something when they'd rejected space colonization for living in mud huts on New Mars.

She entered the galley, feeling exhilarated and exhausted all at once, then noticed the seat by the monitoring station was empty. Roberta was gone. She must have gotten to work on figuring out the problem with the conduits already. No problem there – it meant Kelly could head straight to the immersion chamber and dive right in. She clonked the spacesuit helmet down on the table, set the liquids processor to fast-produce a glass of synthetic orange juice, down it in three gulps and headed for the chamber. She paused briefly in front of Roberta's room, remembering the missing tampons, then decided it would be bad form to snoop through her belongings after she'd agreed to take over her shift. Maybe now that there was real hope for rescue their relationship would come to a turning point, and she could just ask her up front.

Upon reaching the immersion chamber, Kelly grabbed the visigoggles from the place she'd left them earlier and plunked herself down on the hoverchair in the middle of the room. It dipped under her weight as the repulsors adjusted their output to keep it floating in the air, an advanced feature meant to absorb any unwitting spasms the user might experience during the sim. Again she didn't bother taking off the suit. There wasn't much point – once the visigoggles linked with her neural implants and manifested the vidworld for her to experience, her physical awareness of her body would be altered to match the sim's parameters. There were no spacesuits on Ancient Island, so she wouldn't be able to sense that she had it on. She'd go to the trouble of taking it off when she went to bed later, if even then.

Kelly pressed the visigoggles into place and flicked them on. There was an electric hum as the booting sequence initiated. She settled back into the hoverchair and tried to relax. Then there was a flash, followed by colours pouring into the empty void before her eyes. She watched as those colours took shape; greens filled out leafy canopies, blues streaked overhead to paint the skies, browns swirled about her feet to fashion the earth. In a moment she found herself standing in the middle of a deep thicket. It was a familiar place – the Island only had a handful of spawn points. This one was a short walk from the lake.

Kelly looked down at her hands, then her clothes. Her skin was painted with blue swirls and a scratchy woven tunic covered her forearms. She gave a sigh of satisfaction. The druidess had returned.

She started down the path, in no hurry to reach the lakeshore. In truth, she was reluctant to arrive there. It would mean that a decision needed to be made. As long as she remained in the woods she could absorb the scents, allow the sunlight to slip through the gaps in the trees and warm her face. But the path always ended up in the same place, and there was only so far she could wander from it before she'd bounce against the invisible walls. Jefferson had intended the sim experience to draw the viewer to the lake, for reasons Kelly had not yet uncovered. She'd tried peering into the bottom of the lakebed, thinking there might be a treasure somewhere down there, or a cave system to explore. All she'd found was sand and weeds. She'd tried circumventing the lake via the shoreline, but she could only walk so far before, again, she bumped against a wall. She'd walked the opposite way, deeper into the forest, thinking she might come across something of interest. The forest appeared never-ending. Most often she simply rambled, crossing hilltops and valleys, soaking in the sublime beauty of a world untouched by human hands.

Yet it was inevitable that she would reach the lake at some point. She emerged through some bushes and found it waiting for her just beyond a sandy beach. Slow ripples moved across the water, pushed along by a soft breeze that whispered through her hair. As always, the lake's far end was obscured by a low-hanging fog. She'd never managed to penetrate it and discover what lay on the other side. For all she knew, Jefferson had placed the fog there to hide the fact that he'd never programmed anything to lie beyond it. But she had a hard time believing that, considering how thoroughly realized the rest of the immersion was. He'd designed a goat AI, after all. Her druidess's robes itched as if they really were crawling with fleas. It followed that the fog's presence was purposeful.

But she'd never know for sure if she couldn't swim. She'd never really had the opportunity to learn, being raised on an asteroid mining colony. Water was a precious resource aboard Sigma-station, not something for recreation. The megacorp that operated the facility hadn't built any public pools or baths for their workforce. Even though Kelly had traded the mining life years ago for freelance work, drifting from outpost to outpost, the amenities available to her hadn't improved. She'd only made planetfall once or twice in her life, and those had been barren rocky worlds with nothing to offer besides toxic gas, extreme temperatures and uranium deposits. So when she'd signed up to fly with Wayne and his crew and learned that they had a state-of-the-art immersion chamber on board for personal use, she'd been overjoyed. Jefferson's interest in sim-programming had only sweetened the deal. She was an eager sim-tester, willing to explore each new world he created and play around in it until something glitched and she fell through the earth or some such. Their arrangement had worked that way for months; she helped him find and squish bugs, while he provided her with opportunities to experience things she'd never thought she would: tai-chi, fly-fishing, zero-grav omnidirectional basketball, barista training.

All that had ended with the crash. One by one the crew had been picked off, until only Kelly and Roberta remained. A shiver ran through her as she pictured each of their faces, imaging their reflections in the water. Wayne, Davis, Julie, Jefferson, Kyle, and so many more. She owed it to them, she thought, to keep on living. To tell their stories to the world when she managed to get back to civilization. Give some solace to their families, letting them know how each of them fought to survive – except maybe Davis, who'd panicked and tried to abandon them in one of the escape pods by himself. The Sludge had been waiting, and Wayne had given the order to jettison the pod with him inside. He'd got what he wanted, in a way. Maybe that was what she could tell his parents when she saw them.

Kelly shook her head, then stretched her arms up to the sky. She needed to clear her mind if she was going to dive; it wouldn't help her nerves to have the faces of the dead drifting in and out of her consciousness. She scaled the cliff face west of the lake, feeling the grit of the rock in her hands, the rushing breeze in her hair and nostrils. Better to focus on those things. Be a druidess – one with nature, at peace with the universe.

From the top of the cliff, she peered down into the water. It was a fair distance across the lake to the fog. She practiced the proper arm movements, warming herself up. She'd managed to stay afloat for a few minutes before, through trial and error. There wasn't anyone around to coach her. It all came down to how relaxed she was – tensing her muscles only made her sink. She kicked her legs out, trying to loosen the tendons. But this was just her dithering, really. She exhaled, then pulled the scratchy robes over head. She stood naked on the precipice, the wind nipping at her naked skin. Nothing left to do but jump.

So she jumped. She clamped her arms against her chest and clenched her legs together, becoming like a human needle piercing the fabric of the water. She plunged downward and knifed through the water, bitter cold enveloping her entire body. She kicked and pushed back to the surface, then re-emerged, sputtering water from her nose and mouth. She coughed and spun around to beat her bearings. The fog was still there, across the lake. A rush of exhilaration flowed through her veins – she'd actually jumped! She'd been too nervous the times she'd tried before. It had to be the knowledge that rescue was coming that emboldened her. She felt like she could do anything now. The terror was at an end, and she was free to enjoy herself without having to worry about water supplies, electrical outages, oxygen reserves, or undead crewmates.

The druidess began paddling out to where the fog touched the surface of the water. She floundered and slipped under the water a number of times, yet she found she always had the strength to pull herself back up and keep going. It even felt invigorating, though a burning kind of invigoration; her muscles straining, her lungs heaving, the cold stinging her skin. The techniques she'd taught her herself seemed to be working. She gave a little shout of jubilation as she turned back and saw the distance she'd covered – she had to be half-way across already! She ploughed on, gulping water once or twice by accident. The fog loomed closer and closer. She thought she could see something on the other side, or maybe in the midst of it. A shoreline, maybe, or an island. But she felt certain that there was indeed a secret within the fog – something Jefferson had hidden in there for her to find. All the embarrassing failures she'd had teaching herself the proper strokes, all the frightening moments she'd endured as she'd sank below the surface and the simulation entered hard-shutdown, all the strain and effort she was putting herself through now – they were all worth it.

Then, there was a bright flash, and the world vanished into darkness. The sensation of floating in water vanished with it, and she was just floating – weightless, as she did in space. Kelly thought it was a glitch at first. She twisted her head around, trying to figure out where she was, if she'd been suspended in some kind of loading-screen stasis, when she felt a force prying at her temples. Then light came flooding in, and she saw she was staring up at the ceiling of the immersion chamber. Her eyes fluttered as she scanned the room. Roberta was standing over her, holding the visigoggles in her hand.

"Roberta?" she croaked. "What the hell's going on?"

Roberta said nothing. She tossed the visigoggles aside and hefted what appeared to be a thick cord.

"Hey, those are fragile!" Kelly shouted. She was still bleary-eyed from the light of the chamber flashing into view, so she couldn't make out what Roberta was doing with the cord. She tried to sit up from the hoverchair and found that she couldn't. She tried to lift her arms, as if to pry herself out of it, but they wouldn't move either.

"Stop struggling," Roberta said. "You'll only hurt yourself."

Kelly blinked profusely, the room coming into focus at last. She traced the line of the cord Roberta was holding. It led from her hands, across the floor, and up to her waist. She gave a cry as she realized why her arms couldn't move – the cord was wrapped around her in several loops, binding them to her sides. She wriggled to try and loosen them, but they only clenched more tightly. She gazed up at Roberta in dumb bewilderment.

"You tied me up?"

"It's for your own good," Roberta said, staring back down at her.

Kelly twisted violently in the hoverchair. Because she was still wearing the suit she didn't feel the cord biting into her skin, but it restricted her all the same.

"Don't, Kelly. These are hyperfiber cables from the ship's electrical wiring. You can't get out of them."

"Hyperfiber cables? Where the hell – then take them off, Roberta! Let me go!"

There was no answer. Terror welled up in Kelly's heart as she beheld Roberta's emotionless face. The woman's eyes were cold and dead, like those of a spider impassively witnessing the futile struggle of captured prey.

Roberta pulled on her end of the cable. The entire hoverchair drifted forward a few inches. Roberta nodded, then turned and began pulling the chair, with Kelly in it, toward the immersion chamber door.

"Roberta," Kelly said, giving up on trying to free herself for the moment, "can you hear me? Have you gone insane? Let me out of this!"

"It's not me who's lost it, Kelly. I had to protect myself."

"Protect yourself? From what?"

"You, obviously."

"What, you think I'm dangerous?" In her panic, a demented sort of laugh escaped her lips. She cut herself off, cringing at the sound. It certainly didn't make her sound harmless. "You're the one who tied me up! What are you even planning on doing? Toss me overboard? Make me walk the plank?"

"I'm taking you to the cryogenic freezer chambers."

Kelly felt the blood drain from her face.

"You're gonna freeze me?"

Roberta gave her a glance. "First you, then me."

They passed through the door and entered the corridor. Roberta tugged her along behind her in the direction of the galley. Kelly kicked out her feet, but the shock-absorbing features of the hoverchair nullified the effort. There was nothing she could do but be dragged behind her like a legless puppy on a leash. She had maybe two minutes before they reached the freezers – two minutes to talk her way out of this before she ended up on ice, permanently.

"Roberta, listen to me. You've gotta let me go. I'm not crazy, alright? We can talk this out." There was only silence save for the clomping of Roberta's boots against the grav-panels. "Seriously, I'm not. I saw the transmission signal! Why would I make that up?"

"I don't think you're making it up," Roberta said.

"What? You don't? Then why–"

"I believe you *think* you saw it. But you've lost touch with reality.

You think there's a way out of this – that we're still gonna be rescued even when we're lightyears deep in dead space. You've convinced yourself it's possible and you're not going to let anyone make you see reason." She hunched her shoulders as she switched the cord from left to right. "So I've got no choice. If you had your way, you'd go on like this forever. You'd slip further and further into your fantasies, leaving me to deal with the Sludge myself, just to keep us alive. And I don't think it's worth it anymore."

"Not worth being alive? Roberta, if you go in that freezer, you're not coming back out! When someone finds the ship, they won't be able to detect our life signatures if we're frozen."

"I'm willing to take that chance. Way I see it, we're dead either way. At least this way I won't get turned into…whatever the others became." She flashed Kelly a look over her shoulder. "This way, the Sludge doesn't win."

"The Sludge doesn't win if we get rescued!" Kelly said, straightening herself up so she could meet her eyes. "What if someone really does find us and tries to come aboard? What if the Sludge gets them too and wipes out a whole 'nother ship? You ever think of that? Would our lives really be worth losing all those others?"

Kelly clenched her eyes shut and shook her head. She couldn't believe this was happening – on the verge of salvation, and Roberta wanted to abandon all hope! They only needed to last a few more days, weeks maybe, but rescue was coming. She'd seen the transponder signal flashing. She'd seen the blue light. There had to be some way she could make Roberta believe her.

By now they'd reached the galley. Roberta pushed some of the furnishings aside to make room for the hoverchair as she dragged her along behind. Panic swelled within her as she watched the door to the cryo-chambers loom closer and closer. She began thrashing her head from side to side, emitted a primal roar of fury and terror. None of it fazed Roberta – she carried on toward the door like a soldier marching off to the frontline.

Then, just as Kelly was passing the table, she noticed something glisten on its surface. The space helmet was still sitting right where she'd left it. A sort of thick, mucus-like coating was slathered across its side. The trail ran along the tabletop, then vanished at the edge. Kelly craned her neck and thought she could see it continue along the floor before disappearing behind the water recycler.

Her eyes snapped forward as she realized what the source of the trail was. All she saw were the normal features of the galley, and Roberta ahead of her.

"Wait, Roberta – watch out! Sludge!"

Roberta looked up. It was an instinctual act, but exactly the one she shouldn't have done. Kelly saw a small black blob drop from the ceiling above Roberta's head. Roberta was quick enough to leap back a step, but the blob still landed on her shoulder. It quivered there for a moment as Roberta shrieked and slapped it away. Some of its body splattered on the floor, but the remainder crawled its way up her neck. She dropped the cord and clawed at it, raking her nails across the skin. The Sludge stretched itself out, becoming slender like a worm. It evaded her and reached up to her ear, then squeezed itself inside.

Roberta gave a piercing cry and tore at her ear. Kelly could only watch in horror as she careened across the galley, knocking over chairs and crashing into the center table. It toppled on its side, and she went with it. She pulled on the cord as she fell, dragging Kelly out of the hoverchair and down onto the floor with her. She writhed there for a few seconds, hacking like a drowning woman. Then, she went absolutely still.

The galley went silent. All Kelly could hear was the thundering of her own heart. She lay in place for a few moments, wondering if this was the end of the ordeal. But she knew better. Already she could hear low groaning sounds coming from Roberta's corpse. The Sludge acted fast – she had a few minutes before the reanimated Roberta was coming back for her. Kelly tried to worm her way forward, testing her bindings, but they held strong.

There was a shuffling sound from behind the table. Roberta was rising, slowly, black dribble falling from her open mouth. Kelly gave a stifled cry and she tried to tear herself free. She kicked out her feet and knocked over the water recycler, blocking her view of Roberta for a moment. It wouldn't last – Roberta's powerful muscles would be able to heave it out of the way almost effortlessly. She wriggled on her belly for the doorway leading out to the corridor they'd just come through.

Something grabbed her ankle. She screamed and kicked back as hard as she could, catching Roberta full in the face. The corpse grunted and fell back, slamming into the wide viewing window. She recovered right away and launched herself at Kelly with a mad roar.

Lying prone on the floor, there was only one thing Kelly could think of doing to protect herself; she saw Roberta sailing through the air toward her, she bent back her legs, then kicked them upward just as the corpse was about to land on top of her. Her feet caught Roberta in the stomach. Kelly rolled back, keeping her legs out straight to prevent Roberta from clawing her. The momentum from Roberta's jump carried her forward, throwing her right over Kelly and back toward the doorway. She landed in a crumpled heap on the threshold. Kelly scrambled across the floor, trying to find purchase so she could right herself and run.

Roberta's corpse coughed up a heap of Sludge and began to rise again. Kelly moaned in terror. There was no way she could outrun the thing as long as she was still bound. She closed her eyes and braced herself for the pain.

An explosion rang out, buffeting Kelly with hot air. She screamed and opened her eyes to see Roberta's corpse wreathed in flames. She was still staggering forward, toward Kelly, her skin charred and peeling. Then she collapsed, not three feet from where Kelly lay. The flames quickly spread to the table, the machinery, the countertops. Drips of black Sludge oozed from the corpse and sizzled in the heat.

Deep in shock, Kelly could hardly process all that had just happened. She glanced up at the doorway and saw the flamethrower device Roberta had rigged up. It must have sensed the Sludge presence within her as she'd crossed the threshold and detonated. In doing so it had set fire to the rest of the galley, but Kelly could understand now why Roberta would have wanted that – a scorched earth policy. If the Sludge ever made it as deep into their territory as the galley, there wasn't any point in going on. Better to burn what was left of the ship and take the Sludge down with them.

But that had been Roberta's belief. Kelly wasn't dead yet. Even with the flames roaring about her, the smoke choking out the room's oxygen, she still had time to find a way out.

It was then that she remembered the laser-cutter. It was still in the pocket, disassembled. Kelly flipped herself onto her back, crunched her shoulder into her neck, and bit at the pocket flap. Her teeth found a grip and she managed to shred the material loose. The laser-cutter components tumbled onto the floor and slid somewhere behind her. Unable to see what she was doing with her hands, she pawed the ground until she could feel the laser-cutter in her one palm, and the battery in the other. She slammed them together and flipped the ignition. Arching her back to avoid slicing herself, she managed to cut through the hyperfiber cables binding her wrists. Instantly, the entire cord went limp. She pulled herself free and got to her feet, hacking on smoke. She stumbled forward a few feet to where she knew a fire extinguisher to be stashed below the countertop, but the scorching heat pushed her back. In dismay, she looked about the galley. There was no saving it. These flames would spread uncontrollably and consume what was left of the entire ship.

Kelly looked at the helmet on the ground and grit her teeth. She kicked it over, checking that there weren't any more piggy-backing Sludge piles. It was clean, and by now more than a little singed. She snatched it up and slammed it on her head. The suit's oxygen pumped into her lungs, allowing her to breathe freely. She checked the tank levels – fourteen hours. It would be enough. It had to be.

The suit protected her from the worst of the flames as she crashed her way through the burning galley and out into the main corridor. She thundered down the service ladder to where the airlock was located, emergency sirens wailing in her ears, red warning lamps flashing madly. She leapt into the airlock and sealed the door behind her just as a gas pipe exploded and flames tore along the ceiling. A minute later the airlock door to open space unsealed, and she pushed herself out into zero gravity. She wasted no time activating the jetpack system and flying a safe distance from the ship's exterior. Once the flames travelled along the gas pipes and reached the fuel stores, the entire thing would blow. She couldn't stop that – not even if the rest of the crew had still been alive. But that didn't mean it was all over.

She steered the suit along the ship's outer hull and up toward the communications tower. She had to dodge around floating debris from the initial crash as she made her way there. There would be millions of tiny pieces like these sailing through space at thousands of kilometers a second when the reactor blew – she needed to be as far away as possible when that happened to avoid being pierced by shrapnel. But there was still a chance.

As she came to the top of the tower, she scanned the various radio dishes and antennae that topped it. From her many service missions alongside Ollie and the others she thought she knew which one to look for. It was there, hidden in the middle of a large array. She hovered above the selected dish and activated her laser-cutter. She sliced speedily, but with care. There wasn't any time to waste with the ship now a literal time bomb beneath her feet. She cut the receiver dish free, along with the electrical cables connecting it to the ship. It stopped revolving as soon as it was separated from its power source, but she didn't worry about that. She disassembled the laser-cutter again, withdrawing the battery. She hesitated letting go of the … - this little tool had saved her life today in more ways than one – but she didn't have the time or the space to be sentimental. She left it floating there above the tower as she clenched the receiver dish in both hands and jettisoned off into the blackness of empty space.

Once she'd reached maximum acceleration, she decoupled the jetpack from her suit and swiveled around so it was at her chest. It was a rough wiring job, connecting the receiver dish to the pack, but she knew a few tricks to make the electronics interface. She attached the battery from the laser-cutter into the makeshift device, and the dish came to life. She breathed a huge sigh of relief and even laughed to herself – a laugh tainted by fatigue and anxiety, but a laugh all the same. She held out the device in front of her and clipped one of the loose cables to the arm of her suit. She typed in a few commands on the rudimentary keypad to bring up the recording interface.

"Testing, one two. Testing, one two."

A wavy line ran across the screen, indicating that the device had picked up the audio from the comm link in her helmet. The tepid smile on her face grew a fraction wider.

"This is Kelly Van Der Meer, ensign aboard the *Gallant Strider.* I've been forced to abandon ship. There's no one left on board – do not attempt a flyby. There's a – or, will be – a massive debris field after a cataclysmic explosion. Total system failure. But I'm still here. I've retrofitted some old equipment to serve as a broadcasting device. I'll be beaming out my signal for the next–" She paused to check the oxygen indicator on her suit. "–The next thirteen and a half hours. I'll be waiting for you to come and pick me up."

She shut off the recording and set the device to transmit. Her message would be beaming out on all frequencies now. Whoever it was that had responded to their distress call was bound to pick it up. When they did, they'd have her coordinates in real time, as the transmission was set to loop, meaning every few seconds it would update her exact location in space. It would only require her rescuer to track her movement, match her speed, then she could be brought aboard safely. All she needed to do now was wait.

An idea struck her as she drifted through space. The stars were so distant that they didn't appear to be moving at all, even though she was flying toward them at several hundred kilometers an hour. It was almost like swimming, she realized, or treading water, at least. If she wanted to she could move in any direction – up, down, forward, backward. She chuckled at the thought. She lifted her arms and began to cycle them in front-crawl fashion. She leaned forward and kicked her legs as if she were submerged and propelling herself forward. It was even easier than it had been in the simulation, because empty space did nothing to resist her movements. The utter blackness, which once she had found so unnerving, took on a new quality altogether. It was like an ocean; dark and shapeless, unknowable in its vastness, yet still traversable. Those stars out there were more than flickering lights – they were islands. No invisible walls or dense fog prevented her from reaching them. She could keep on swimming like this, forever, until she reached the distant shore.

BEYOND THE FARTHEST REACH – PAUL CARROLL

"Impact in twenty."

The voice belonged to an operator outside of Paris, a city now encased in a defensive bubble of ionised energy and surrounded by a military presence that hadn't been seen since the 20th century. The only difference was that Paris was now under the protection of all those both in-and-outside the barrier, a united human force that had been established across the globe to protect major cities, Ecostations and ports.

Standing in the fields that spread out across central France was the giant mechanical suit, Geryon, of the United Global Defence Forces, piloted by Sgt. Sebastian Wells. Sebastian was one of only a few pilots who could properly handle Geryon, out of still only a few dozen people worldwide who could handle a mech suit of any design. They had a few unofficial classes, from brawlers to artillery, with Geryon operating in a class of its own, a mech equipped with wings and thrusters, built for speed. It had been painted in dark greens and blacks, best suited for combat at night, but still capable of holding its own in a battle.

Geryon fought just as Sebastian had been trained, with retractable blades on its arms for swift assaults and a pulse cannon on its chest that allowed for an explosive means of escape if things got too dicey. The pulse cannon was a one-shot blast, requiring too much cooldown time and energy to be utilised multiple times in a battle without tearing Geryon apart.

In the cockpit, Sebastian Wells was strapped into a multiplanar travelator, with motion sensors working to track his movements and allow for seamless combat within and without. It was a change of pace from fighter jets and regular hand-to-hand combat, one that kept his time occupied outside of a few personal days throughout the year, and something that could only loosely be described as a life outside the military. *Too much time working*, his partner had said to him, *not enough time living*.

He shook the thought from his head. "Final systems check," Sebastian said, his comms open to the others on the field that day.

The Western Europe unit of mechs, collectively the Emperors, consisted of a trio named for long-dead rulers of Rome: Augustus, Nero and Claudius. One by one, the pilots sent their affirmations, Raquel Leclert from Nero, Havier Haller from Augustus and Simone Pesce from Claudius.

"Four targets incoming," Haller added.

"Impact in ten," came the voice of the operator.

Sebastian let out a deep breath, slow and steady. "Okay Geryon, let's do this."

First Contact had been an event to celebrate. Second Contact had been one to fear.

A decade ago, the first and only warship from the alien species that identified itself as the Flaran blazed a path through space from just beyond the Asteroid Belt, utilising technology that humankind could only dream of to close the gaps in space that made interplanetary travel infeasible. It burned with cosmic radiation for a week when it crash-landed on French soil, tearing a chasm across the plains that would never fully seal.

The military response had been swift, and the public panic difficult to manage, but the message the Flaran brought with them was one of fear and dread. Though their own defences were compromised from their landing, they were more than capable of withstanding most of Earth's weapons. Whatever had damaged the Flaran ship had been much more dangerous than anything developed thus far.

The issue with the Flaran, beyond the blazing trail they had left in their wake, was their appearance. They were cephalopodic in nature, resembling octopods to some degree, but with bodies larger than elephants and arms that stretched out further still. They floundered out of their ships, struggling at first with the atmosphere, but not so deterred that they didn't make their first attempt at communication, blasting the closest humans with a telepathic wave that knocked most of them out. Where over a thousand people had been hit, only a few dozen remained on their feet, and it was their protests that kept the Flaran safe from further assaults.

They were not the threat.

The question on everyone's lips was finally communicated to the Flaran by one of the military scientists who had been capable of hearing the Flaran's first message. "What was so bad that you had to come here?"

The Flaran commune shuddered at the question, the thought echoing through their ship, and they responded with a request, and an image that had been burned into their psyches: *Don't let the Baxoon settle on Earth.*

Part of the relocation of Sebastian Wells and Geryon to Europe had included a permanent residence for his father, Ernest Wells. He was on bedrest in what could loosely be described as a nursing home on the outskirts of Paris, just inside the civilian section of the barrier. Sebastian visited him as often as he could, though without any sort of regularity; in the years since the first Baxoon assault, it had become increasingly difficult for people in Sebastian's position to make any arrangements for personal time. It was a luxury the Earth couldn't afford.

"I just can't believe you want to marry this guy," his father wailed. Ernest Wells had not become more bitter with his illness; it had always been his default state of mind, for as long as Sebastian could remember.

"It's called love, dad," Sebastian responded. "Maybe you've forgotten how it feels before you marry someone, but some of us still value the symbol of marriage in a relationship."

Ernest harrumphed. "But I'm not going to get any grandkids out of this one. What about Emma? I'm sure she'd be happy to date a strapping guy like you."

Across the room, Emma's cheeks burned. She was Ernest's nurse, his primary carer and the person responsible for making sure he took his medication every morning, afternoon and night. She was several years Sebastian's junior, and very much the sort of trophy wife that Ernest would have liked to pass his son onto, if not for a few obvious complications.

"I'm going to try pretend I didn't hear you pawning me off," Emma called, keeping her back turned on the Wells men.

"Honestly," Sebastian muttered. "Dad, for the last time, myself and Idris are a couple. It's not a phase. It's not an act of rebellion. This isn't the twentieth century. We're in love, and we're getting married."

"And you haven't set a date," Ernest added. "I just don't get why you'd want to get married during all of this, anyway. What, you going to have that Flaran beast he works with attend the reception? Or maybe you'd like to wear your suit to the ceremony in case of a Baxoon invasion escaping the radar."

Emma swerved around with a cup of water and Ernest's pills in her hands. "Your medication, Ernie. It's the fun stuff this morning." She waited until the old man had his mouth full and his attention preoccupied to add, "I think it's sweet that you're getting married. But if I can offer one bit of advice, Seb, act on it soon. Love is absolutely something worth fighting for in the midst of all this chaos, but at some point you have to stop fighting and start living, or it all starts to lose its value."

Ernest tried to agree, to use the nurse's words against his son, against the wedding, but he was cut off by a beeping from Sebastian's wrist watch. "Sorry dad, I'm supposed to meet Idris for coffee. I'll catch you soon, okay? And try not to torture Emma too much."

A daily coffee with Idris was the only thing Sebastian really had that felt normal. It didn't matter if it was early or late, since the start of their relationship it had been a constant, shifting between work schedules and observation shifts and training programmes, and not always in-person if circumstances got in the way. Always in the same café, a fabrication of normality in the research lab where Idris worked.

Sebastian was almost always late, the military man of the pair, always pulled away at a moment's notice just as things seemed to be going his way. Idris had long gotten over it. Instead he just waited at their table, coffees waiting and steaming, ready to order a fresh cup if Sebastian ran especially late, and always wearing a smile on his face when he finally showed up. "I can always tell when you've been to see your father," Idris remarked. "You get resting serial killer face."

Sebastian rolled his eyes. "You've been telling that joke for six years."

"And I'll tell for sixty more if you let me."

"This is going to be a wedding conversation, isn't it?"

"We have to have one eventually," Idris insisted. "You proposed to *me*, remember? Just look, I've been highlighting some venues, getting some costs pencilled in. There's this cute chateaux in Bordeaux we can rent out, and all of our guests will have their own space. We can have wine, and sit by a pool, and watch the sun set over the Atlantic. Weddings happen there all the time. It'll be a peaceful little weekend, and-"

"You think I have a weekend to spare in the middle of all of this?"

Idris sighed. "Well, it was this or a quicky at town hall and a two-week honeymoon in the Caribbean. I figured the shorter affair might be more appealing to you."

The phrase *a quicky at town hall* was not uncommon in their wedding plans. Idris liked to use it as a means of breaking down any objections that Sebastian might have to picking a date. Not that it was ever really what Idris wanted. Sebastian knew that too well. For as long as they'd known each other, Idris had been a romantic. He wanted the big wedding. He wanted to show off his husband to people in a ceremony that meant something.

And, he knew that Sebastian would never go for it without a little bit of pressure.

"I just think we need to set a date, get things moving, okay?" Idris added. "I was talking with Adam about it this morning, and he agrees. With everything going on in the world, and all the issues with your father's health, we don't really know when the right time will be."

Sebastian had long-since gotten used to the mention of Adam, to the point that he had stopped flinching at the name when it came up in the middle of conversations about their relationship. He wasn't another man, not in the traditional sense, so there was no romantic rivalry to be concerned with. But he wasn't human, either.

Adam was one of the few surviving Flaran to have landed on Earth, the father to the first generation of terrestrially-born Flarans, and the military's best source of information on the invading Baxoon. Even if the facility where he lived was technically privately owned.

Idris had been among the first to speak with Adam, and had become the military contact on Flaran technology that could be communicated effectively by way of Flaran telepathy. There was still a lot of speculation about how it worked, but without a cadaver to pick apart, it wasn't likely that people would really understand *how* the Flaran did it.

All Sebastian knew was that it was meant to be an intimate experience, a link that couldn't be severed once it had been established. Idris and Adam were bound to each other in a way that Sebastian could never stand up to, and though there was a limit to the range of Adam's telepathic capabilities, both Idris and Adam always knew where the other was, and occasionally felt flickers of strong emotion from the other side. It wasn't a unique connection, and Idris wasn't Adam's only link; he – if the Flaran could be reduced to binary genders – had multiple human partners and a link with every other Flaran alive on Earth.

"You're doing that thing again," Idris said to him, drawing him back into the conversation. "Tell me what's wrong."

"It's nothing," Sebastian grumbled, absently stirring his coffee to keep Idris from making eye contact. He knew that he would give it all away if they locked eyes, that Idris could read him clear as day. They didn't need a telepathic link for that.

A beep from his wrist distracted him, a signal that only ever meant one thing: the next wave of Baxoon invaders was incoming. Their ships were fast, but only survived the journey by functioning as solo transports, skipping through the asteroid belt and whizzing across space towards the Earth. Idris had once described the wormhole they travelled through as being a hole made solid in the fabric of reality, too small for the type of ships that the Flaran had described descending onto their planet, too tight a squeeze for something that might pose an intergalactic threat.

It bought them time, to know where to look beyond the inner circle of the solar system, a place to focus the planet's defences and project the trajectory of the incoming ships to rally the military on time.

"They have other soldiers," Idris reminded him firmly.

Sebastian shuffled in his seat. "Right."

"Tell me what's wrong, Seb. You always try to put this conversation off, and I'm beginning to think the wedding isn't the issue." He reached out and placed a hand on Sebastian's, soft skin pulling Sebastian out of his head and back to the table, a sense of familiarity and comfort that he'd never found with anyone.

"What do you see in Adam that you can't see in me?" he asked. Idris flinched, and almost pulled his hand away, but Sebastian took hold of it, lightly. *Stay with me*, he seemed to say. "You open up to him. I know you do, or you wouldn't be discussing our wedding plans with him. He's not just a research specimen to you, is he?"

Idris's eyes fell to the table. "It's different with him, and it always has been. But the Flaran, they don't do romance. They don't do love. Their whole civilisation is built on intellect and emotion. They breed for the sake of perseverance of their race, without discrimination.

They don't have weddings or monogamy or marriages.

"When I talk to Adam, he tells me about their way of life, how things were and how they are now. He shares technology, as much as he can. You've seen the Ecostations. You pilot a mech suit. You can see what my work with Adam, and what others' work with the other Flaran, has led to. We share cultural insights with them, too, so they can understand their new home, and part of that is… well, we tell them about our personal lives."

"But why?" Sebastian asked.

Idris's dark eyes gave nothing away, and he was saved from answering for a moment when Sebastian's watch beeped again.

"I can leave," he said to Idris.

"Stay. Please." Idris sighed. "Adam can see into my head. Since the first telepathic wave, he's been buried in there. They don't do that with other species, not regularly. Not that they've encountered much else out there. But it helps both of us to be open. If we shut out a part of our lives that means something to us, the connection… it grows weaker? I guess? I was hesitant for a long time, and our progress was slow. But when I told him about love, and how I feel about you, and what I want our wedding to be like, and what it feels like when we both get to shut off for a little while…"

The watch beeped again.

"They have other pilots," Sebastian said.

Idris smiled, lips quivering. "Not like you," he said. "Go. Save the world again. We can pick this up later."

They kissed, quickly and gently, as Sebastian left. His coffee sat steaming, untouched, on the table.

"Impact in five."

Geryon and the Emperors steadied themselves. Between the four of them, they had several dozen kills against the invading Baxoon, and had learned to work together based on each other's strengths and weaknesses.

Nero was their main artillery, boasting shoulder cannons that made short work of the less-armoured Baxoon. Leclert had long since made it her responsibility to thin the Baxoon numbers wherever possible. The targeting systems that had come from Flaran technology - and the weapons that worked better with humanity's designs than Flaran degrees of pacifism had allowed - ensured most battles against invading forces were short and painless, that the Baxoon couldn't get much footing on Earth, or spread to the cities.

Nero had been difficult to work with. Almost every pilot that could handle a mech had tried to use it, but the machine had a temperament that couldn't be bested by masculine aggressiveness. The Flaran technology that allowed the mechs to work the way they did had instilled too much of a personality to the machines, enough that they wouldn't perform quite so well without the right pilot in the cockpit.

Whatever Raquel Leclert had done to earn the trust of Nero, she was the only person alive who could pilot it, and wore that as a badge of honour in the military. No one could doubt the role of a woman in the United Global Defence Forces.

Alongside Nero, Augustus and Claudius worked as close-range fighters. Augustus wielded a mace in lieu of a right arm, while Claudius was equipped with two large blades on each arm, acting as knives with which it could stab at the Baxoon. They worked in tandem to disrupt the movements of the invading giants, dismantling weapons and tearing open wounds with relative ease, leaving them open for absolute defeat either at the hand of Nero's cannons, or from further coordinated attacks. Havier and Simone had been working together for the duration of the Baxoon invasion, and while both were now getting on in age as far as military pilots were concerned, neither was ready to hand in the towel yet.

"Impact made."

"Four targets incoming," said Commander Haller, from within Augustus. Haller was a Spanish soldier, older than any of the others, and more than ready to take the fight up close and personal. "Augustus and Claudius can handle the lumbering one. It's big, but it'll fall easily enough. Nero, please direct your firepower on the top-heavy Baxoon. They're slow, and unlikely to be able to dodge your blasts. We'll provide assistance as soon as possible."

Sgt Wells chimed in. "That leaves the Skitter to me." Skitters were what Wells and his colleagues called the shorter, quicker Baxoon. They were still giants as far as people were concerned, but the way they moved and held themselves, they appeared smaller on the battlefield.

"Sergeant, please remain diligent. The fourth shuttle looked larger than the previous Skitter pods," the operator added.

"Copy," Sebastian replied, waiting for the first sight of the Skitter. Bigger and faster might be an issue, he thought, but he'd handled worse in the past. And that wasn't including Idris's family.

The Baxoon did not look alike, except for their size. Even then, that was inconsistent. They were vaguely humanoid, with a few variants in physiology; some had additional arms, or extra legs, or multiple heads. Some had tails. One that landed in Asia had flown on enormous bat wings. The Flaran told them that they were more alike on the inside than the outside, that they had the same sort of psychic signature and the same bloodlust, and that when they spawned it was from the same pits. The details were vague on how they knew, though Sebastian had long since wondered exactly how docile the

Flaran really were.

The current set of invaders were a mishmash of monstrosities. The lumbering giant was almost as wide as it was tall, padded out by fat and muscle and layers of thick, discoloured skin. It was like an ogre, violet as it was violent, with enormous tusks erupting out of its mouth. One of its arms was bound in spiky metal, while the other glistened under the light of several bands of light. While the Baxoon were a brutish group, mostly relying on their size and strength for combat, they had a few weapons that matched the Flaran technology for skill.

A pair of top-heavy brutes crawled behind, holding themselves upright on an assortment of extra arms and legs. One had two large arms that did more to carry it along than its legs, and a shorter pair that it kept tucked across its chest. The other, a hairy, green beast, simply dragged its arms behind it, leaving ridges in the ground. It drooled constantly, a savage grin on its face.

Sebastian expected a Skitter to scurry along behind them, and one did. But not just one. Three of them made themselves known, dipping in and out of sight as they hurried towards the mechs - and the city full of people on the other side of them, just waiting to be eaten.

Nero's first blast roared across the French plains, turning the sky to darkness as the ambient light struggled against the pulse cannons. Geryon, Augustus and Claudius wasted no time getting closer to their respective targets. The first Skitter, clambering around on all four with arms longer than its legs, crashed forcefully into Geryon before the light of the pulse cannon had even faded. Sebastian was thrown around inside the cockpit, dizzy from the experience of Geryon losing its footing so suddenly.

Without hesitating, he set his boasters to full power and shot into the air, just high enough to escape the Skitter.

"Status report," came a message from Nero.

"All good. Damn thing was faster than usual," he responded. He rounded Geryon's sights back on the Skitter, which had decided to lead its brother in the direction of Nero. Grounded in place for better use of the cannons, Nero was an open target, and the ideal bait. Geryon soared down, winding in a circle overhead, waiting for the right moment to drop.

Twin blades seared through Baxoon flesh and pinned a Skitter to the ground, just before it could launch itself at Nero. Geryon's wings swam out on either side, knocking the other two Skitters away.

Not that Geryon's interjection made much of a difference. Mere seconds after Geryon had planted its weapons inside the Skitter, the second blast from Nero's pulse cannons erupted across the battlefield. Sebastian turned his attention to the other Baxoon, watching through tinted glass as one of the brutes was obliterated, burned to ash and dust and scattered into the wind.

The lumbering giant was already on its knees, bleeding from deep cuts on each ankle, with a dislocated shoulder from a wallop of Augustus's mace. A finishing blow from Claudius's knives up through its skull ended the giant's life, and left three eyes rolling around in its head.

That left the final two Skitters and the second brute. Geryon was quickly entangled with one of the Skitters, while the other found itself on the wrong end of Augustus's mace. It smashed against the ground, bloody ichor splashing across the grass.

A voice rang in the cockpit of Geryon. "Sebastian, can you hear me?"

"Idris, is that you? What are you doing on this line?"

Geryon's right blade jammed into the torso of the Skitter, pinning it in place, but angering it. Baxoon organs weren't like humans'. Sebastian wasn't sure he had hit anything vital, but he knew one thing for sure: he was stuck, with a giant struggling to break free.

"This is an emergency. I've got permission under the military accord relating to vital information from the Flaran with regard to ongoing combat-"

"Idris, I'm kind of busy," Sebastian snapped. With a swipe of his arm, he severed one of the Skitter's particularly wild legs from the body. "Hold on. Augustus, Claudius, my blade's stuck in its chest, and I'm not sure I'll be able to dislodge without giving it an opportunity to take a bite." The Skitter's jaws snapped at the cockpit, as if it could hear him inside. "Assistance required."

"You don't understand, Seb, this is pertinent to the fight you're in now. There are more incoming."

"What did he say?" came Leclert's voice from Nero. "I don't see any, and the operator didn't give us the heads up."

"The operator is blind to them," Idris told her. "Our whole system is blind. We've missed something. The Baxoon, they'll be here in a couple of minutes. You need to regroup. You need backup." He sighed into the microphone, his worries pouring through the comms in each of the mechs. "It was Adam. He spotted the danger. He recognises it. He calls it *Cottus*."

"Is that supposed to mean something to us?" Haller asked, taking a swipe at the Skitter pinned to Geryon's arm. Its head came clean off, bouncing across the ground. Sebastian tossed the body aside, the limbs limp. Haller offered him assistance to his feet. "That was a close one, eh? Now, Mister… Idris you said? What are you talking about? What is this Cottus?"

Sebastian surveyed the battlefield. From his position on the ground, he hadn't seen Nero destroy the remaining Baxoon. All that remained were discarded limbs, blasted clear from the body. He was grateful for the Ecostations that the Flaran had helped them establish across the globe, sources of food and energy that wouldn't destroy the planet. The damage from each invasion fleet from the Baxoon forces was bad enough.

"Operator, can you confirm what Idris has told us?"

They were met with silence, interrupted by a flurry of button-presses pounding through the comms. "Damn it, he's right. Three more bogies incoming, impact imminent. But they're not on our scanners. How did we…"

Sebastian felt like swearing, but kept his mouth shut. He didn't need to take his anger out on the operator, the voice on the other end of the line whose team monitored every invasion force.

"Idris, who is Cottus? What did Adam tell you?"

Sebastian could feel the tension from Idris. "Cottus is the earth-given name for the Baxoon that led the invasion that destroyed the Flaran home planet. It's nastier than anything else you've ever fought, bigger than the other Baxoon, and much more dangerous. Please, Seb, please come home. The defenses will last until backup arrives."

"Backup isn't coming," the operator interjected. "Three other locations across the globe are reporting similarly hidden invasions. There's nothing to spare at the moment."

The Emperors shared a look between them. Pesce spoke up for them. "If we're it, then we go down fighting. Our families are all in danger. If we don't protect Paris, if we don't stop this… this Cottus… then what are we fighting for at all?"

In the cockpit of Geryon, Sebastian just wanted to scream. They needed to know more. They couldn't go into a fight blind. He sighed. "Idris, why did Adam name the Baxoon *Cottus*? You said it was an earth-given name. Does that mean he followed our naming conventions?"

"Only name the biggest nasties that find their way down here," Leclert said, "And name them for our own monsters."

"It's Greek," Idris said, but that was all he got out before a pulse cannon blasted the ground near the Emperors. Cottus had arrived, and he wasn't alone.

Sebastian took to the sky, to better survey the threats, while Nero sent return fire.

It didn't take a psychic link with Adam to know which of the Baxoon was Cottus. It stood half-again as tall as any of the Baxoon they had fought before, towering over its partners on the battlefield, and utterly dwarfing Augustus and Claudius. The mechs struggled to take one of the Baxoon down, their combined might barely enough to drag it away from Cottus. If they were lucky, and smart, they might avoid any more surprise attacks.

The other Baxoon, coated in thick black skin with eyes burning like coals charged Nero. It had horns on its head, two on one side and one the other, a broken beast of war.

That left Geryon to challenge Cottus himself, and the giant was more than ready. Sebastian didn't know many of the names from Greek mythology, but he knew there were only so many giants they might have named a Baxoon after, and this was no mere giant.

"Idris, you didn't mention this thing was covered in hands."

Cottus roared at Geryon, and raised an arm that had lodged itself into the gun from a warship. The searing light from the pulse cannon ripped through Geron's right wing, grounding the mech instantly. Sebastian felt his knees buckle against the impact as he landed hard on the earth.

Across Cottus's entire body, hands grasped blindly for something to crush and to kill. The giant had additional arms, which seemed to follow orders more logically and consistently, and its entire focus was on ripping Geryon to shreds. Suddenly it didn't matter how long Sebastian had been in the mech, or how much they really knew about the Baxoon or the Flaran, or whether he had a wedding date with Idris or that Idris had a relationship with Adam that no one could ever match. The many-armed giant was practically on top of him, and twice his size, and Geryon's main advantage had been removed.

Sebastian slashed out at Cottus, trying to keep some distance from its hands. The cannon in its hand was smoking, worn out from use already, though it was unclear how long they'd be safe from another blast.

He wanted to check in on the others, but he knew if he took his eyes off Cottus that would be it for him. Game over.

Before he could make another move to attack Cottus, Augustus smashed into him, thrown by the other Baxoon. Claudius was quick to follow, leaving the three in a heap.

"Damn it. Haller, Pesce, status report." He was met with silence. "Augustus, Claudius, pilot status reports for Haller, Havier and Pesce, Simone, on the order of Sergeant Sebastian Wells."

The reports displayed themselves on Sebastian's HUD; he barely had time to experience relief that neither of the men was critically injured when a foot crashed through the pile of mechs. Nausea overtook Sebastian as he spun through the air, crashing onto the ground too far from the fight to be of any assistance to Nero. With the other Emperors down, Nero was fighting back Cottus's companions by itself, pulse cannons barely affecting them anymore.

A flash across his HUD pulled Sebastian back to the danger he was in. Geryon had lost a leg. He rolled over, onto his back, just in time to see Cottus standing over him.

"Full power to the chest cannon, Geryon, and eject."

"Sebastian, what are you doing?" Idris called out.

"What I have to. Idris, I'm sorry."

Cottus was illuminated as it stood over Geryon, and the realisation of what Sebastian had initiated came too late. WIthin seconds, the pulse cannon built into Geryon's chest unleashed all remaining power against the giant.

The Baxoon rarely showed their pain, but even Cottus couldn't contain a scream as one of its larger arms was torn from its body. At the same time, the giant was catapulted through the air, clearing a safe spot for Augustus and Claudius to recuperate and reevaluate their approach.

Geryon's head hissed open, and Sebastian stumbled out. The ejection protocol was meant to release him in the middle of a fight, but without full power there were no safety measures to follow, no parachute to attach, nothing to get the pilot away from the danger.

Cottus was not long getting back on his feet, and only Nero was still fighting.

Sebastian heard the crackle of his comm in his ear, faint from the damage taken by Geryon. "Haller, Pesce, it was good serving with you. Please, flee. Live to fight another day."

"Leclert?" Sebastian mumbled. Light began to blaze through Nero's armour, steam spilling onto the ground and crawling like a fog. "Damn it, Raquel, don't do this!"

There was no going back. He knew it. She knew it. Only the Baxoon, who had never seen something like this, didn't know what to expect when the central generator inside Nero exploded. Uncontained and unfiltered, the energy ripped through the two closest Baxoon, and tossed Cottus away. No one heard him land over the sound of Nero's explosion.

No one saw whether Leclert had been able to eject in time.

***

Sebastian's head was still ringing when he came to.

"Where…?"

"Oh thank goodness," Idris said, rushing to his side. Sebastian's senses slowly returned. He was in a hospital, of sorts, likely the infirmary. "A Flaran shuttle picked you up when we saw what happened to Nero. Geryon's too damaged to recover, not with Cottus still in action."

"He's still alive?"

Idris looked away. He could never bear to deliver bad news. "The blast from Nero did a number on him, but yes. At the moment, there are a number of Flaran ships surrounding him, some of the new shuttles they'd been working on. They're containing him, in the only way they really know how to, but they know from when he arrived on their planet that it's only effective in the short term. The moment they're attacked, they'll lose the containment, and we don't know when the next… I'm sorry."

Sebastian reached out for Idris's hand. "I need to go back out there, Idris. We need to put an end to this." Idris took his hand, but he still couldn't meet his eyes. "What happened to Haller and Pesce?"

"Both fine. Like you, receiving treatment, but they weren't exposed like you were. The radiation… they think they've managed to introduce neutralising agents soon enough, but it could have killed you. Sebastian, what were you thinking?"

He gave Idris's hand a light squeeze and sat upright. "I was thinking that maybe I could sacrifice Geryon to stop Cottus. It didn't work. He's tough."

"Did you miss the part where I told you he led the assault on the Flaran? They couldn't beat him on their own planet." He watched Sebastian throw his bedsheets back. "Okay, what are you doing?"

"I told you, I need to go back out there. I need to stop him. I can't let him get near Paris. I can't let him hurt *you*. Heck, I'll even defend my father if I have to."

"You almost died, Seb. You need to rest. You need to recover your strength."

Sebastian leaned forward and kissed Idris on the lips. "You give me strength," he told him. "But if you also have some pants I could wear, that would be great."

Idris rolled his eyes. "You're unbelievable." He gestured to a bag waiting on the floor. "It's the one you packed and left in my office 'in case of emergency'. Not exactly military spec, but I suppose anything is more socially acceptable than naked from the back."

"Like you're complaining," Sebastian teased.

Idris stopped him before he could leave to get changed. "Before you even attempt to go back into a mech, I need you to do something for me."

"Is this really the right time to discuss a wedding date?"

Idris sighed, but a smile crept onto his face. "I wish, but no. I want you to meet Adam. He's seen Cottus in combat before. We need to know if he has any advice on beating him. He's been watching every invasion, and every pilot's approach to fighting the Baxoon. He might have some insights."

Sebastian wasn't exactly happy with the idea of meeting the Flaran. In the beginning, he had been excited about the technology and the opportunities they offered, but the more he learned about their psychic links, the less he trusted them. But Idris was right, and he *had* almost died in his first fight against Cottus. Maybe, he reasoned, now was the time to face one fear in order to better fight another.

***

The facility where Adam lived was home to almost a dozen other Flaran, half of whom belonged to the first generation of Earth-born Flaran. They resided in a communal pool, though they weren't restricted to the water. They were perfectly capable of crossing land, and could survive in the Earth's atmosphere if they needed to. The water was familiar to them, and reduced any strain to adapt to the air so that they could slowly adapt.

Whether because of his age or because of his telepathic abilities, Adam was known in the facility as the Prime Flaran, the father of the new generation and the primary source of knowledge on Flaran and Baxoon technology and culture.

Sebastian had never seen a Flaran in person, never mind a fully grown one like Adam. He found his legs betraying him as he entered the same room with the alien, a disturbingly familiar monster that towered over him and had its arms spread around the lab, coated in silver skin that seemed to glisten under the fluorescent lights. Adam had more than eight limbs, which was the first thing that struck Sebastian as strange. He had expected something that was more or less an octopus, but Adam had more than a dozen primary limbs, and others branching out of some of them so that the alien seemed to be taking root in the room, planting itself like a monstrous tree.

Adam had more eyes than Sebastian could recognise. There were three primary eyes on his head, open and staring at him when he entered the lab. Others opened every now and then across Adam's many limbs, flickerings of colour and surveillance all around the room.

"Adam, I'd like to formally introduce you to my fiancé, Sebastian Wells. Sebastian, this is Adam, the Prime Flaran in the region."

Sebastian felt a pulse press against his skull, a pressure that seemed to come from within and without at the same time. It felt more like anxiety than a language, and it wrapped around his whole mind before recoiling.

"What was that?" he hissed to Idris.

Idris was silent for a moment, staring at Adam, then turned to Sebastian. "He was testing you. When they first arrived, when they reached out to everyone at once, they didn't know what to look for in a human mind. They probed us blind, trying to speak, to warn us, but they were ineffective for most people. They pushed too hard, and they didn't wait for an invitation."

"You invited him in?"

Idris shook his head. "You know that much of what I do here is classified, but I wouldn't have kept that from you. The first wave, none of us had a choice. It was necessary. But everyone else, they were probed first, then asked for permission to form the bond."

"The bond that can't be broken," Sebastian stated. He didn't need to ask. "Okay. If it will help me to keep everyone safe."

Idris didn't need to relay a message for Adam. Though he lacked visible ears and the means to *speak* English, it seemed quite clear that Adam heard and understood everything said around him. Within seconds, the probing pressure returned, and wound its way through Sebastian's head with only a little bit of discomfort. It was like a tentacle, he thought, and then felt a chuckle run through his mind.

"Whoa," he said under his breath. He could see Idris smiling in the corner of his eye. "I never thought…"

Adam's words weren't in a language Sebastian spoke, seemingly coming into his head like music and screams, but he understood the meaning behind it all. He couldn't explain it, though he imagined Idris would know more about it.

"I need to know more about Cottus," he said to Adam.

"You don't need to say it out loud, you know," Idris told him.

"Just think it."

"Does it bother him if I speak?" He felt the answer from Adam himself, *No*. Not so much in the word, but in a sensation. "Then I'll stick with words. For now, at least. Until this stops feeling new."

Idris rolled his eyes and headed towards the door. "Suit yourself. Get acquainted. I've got a call to make." Sebastian raised an eyebrow at him. They weren't psychic, but they could read each other. "You want to go out there and fight Cottus? You're going to need a mech. Trust me on this. And play nice with Adam."

The new mech stood taller than Geryon.

New was technically a stretch, since it had been piloted by someone else in the past, but he had been honourably discharged from the United Global Defence Forces when he had been diagnosed with a rare spinal cancer. His mech had been put in storage, owing to a lack of suitable replacements, and was already based in West Europe.

"I don't know how you managed to pull this one off, Idris," Sebastian had said, staring up at the mech. It had been painted in light greens and shining golds, with an enormous sword attached to the back and a shield on the left arm. "Does it have a name?"

Idris had smiled with pride. "Say hello to Cuchulainn, the Irish Defender. You won't be able to fly in this one, but he packs a bit more of a punch than Geryon, and he's got his own tricks. Energised sword, pulse dampening shield, retractable spear buried in the back, and tougher than anything else on the battlefield at the moment."

Sebastian had been immediately sold on Cuchulainn. "All he needed was a pilot."

Now, standing on the French plains again, with Augustus and Claudius at each side, Sebastian was ready for round two. Cottus may still be bigger, and proportionally more dangerous than any other Baxoon they'd faced, but with a proper soldier on the field they at least stood a chance.

"Idris, can you hear me?"

"Loud and clear, Sebastian."

"When this is over, I need you to do something for me." He could hear the anticipation in Idris's breath. "Contact the chateau in Bordeaux. I think it's time we picked a date."

"Why now?" Idris asked. "Not that I'm complaining."

Sebastian looked at the battlefield where Nero and Leclert had sacrificed themselves for the sake of the others, and then at the cockpit of Cuchulainn. "You're worth fighting for. You've always been worth fighting for. But fighting isn't enough anymore. We need to live our lives, at some point. All of this has to be worth something, right?"

"Just don't die out there," Idris said. There was silence for a moment, and Sebastian was sure that Idris was trying to compose himself. "I love you, Sebastian."

"I love you too, Idris."

A hiss came through the comms. "I hate to interrupt, because I think you guys are really cute together," the operator said, "But we have incoming ships. Visuals only, no scans yet."

"Idris, relay a message to the Flaran holding Cottus down to evacuate. They can't be caught in the middle of the fight. Operator, give me numbers."

"Three, normal sizes as far as we can tell."

Sebastian looked to each of his companions. "Raquel didn't die so we would lose this battle. Can you handle the incoming Baxoon? The Prime Flaran showed me what Cottus is capable of. I think Cuchulainn can take him, but I can't fight the others as well."

"Do it for her," Haller responded.

"We'll take care of the rest," Pesce confirmed.

The Flaran shuttles zoomed past them, followed by the roar of Cottus as he climbed to his feet. His skin was burnt and charred on the left, and some of the smaller arms and many of the clawing hands had gone limp. He was bleeding from the head, though he seemed unbothered by the injury, and more annoyed that the Flaran had kept him imprisoned by their telepathy.

Sebastian drew Cuchulainn's sword, lighting it up with energy not unlike the pulse cannons. The blaze caught Cottus's attention, undivided and filled with rage. "Remember me, asshole?"

The giant charged on Cuchulainn, ignoring Augustus and Claudius as they approached the new arrivals. A heavy swing from Cottus's right arm smashed against the shield, knocking both giant and mech away from each other.

The pulse cannon fired before Sebastian could close the gap again, but he had been ready for it. With only a little bit of difficulty piloting Cuchulainn, he was able to dodge the incoming blast. Earth exploded up around the mech's feet, scattering for hundreds of feet in every direction. Cottus was not one to play around; the wreck of Geryon was proof enough of that. Still, even avoiding the hit had been a teachable moment. Cuchulainn wasn't as responsive to Sebastian's movements as Geryon had been. There was a lot more mass to move about on the battlefield, which Sebastian hoped would at least translate to a heavier punch when it came time to exchange blows.

He was grateful to have met with Adam before the fight, at least. The Flaran's intel on Cottus had shown his patterns of behaviour. The moment the giant thought he might struggle up close, he drew his weapons. Or whatever he could grab and use as a weapon. He had turned the Flaran warships into his own personal artillery while invading the planet. He had stripped them of their best defences. He was a smart, ruthless monster, one that Sebastian had underestimated in the past.

If the Baxoon had been able to sneak past Earth's sensors, it stood to reason that there was more to them than their appearances suggested.

But where the Baxoon had ruthless intellect and the strength to back it up, the Flaran had cunning and the means to share their knowledge in a way that couldn't be matched. The moment Sebastian recognised that a gap had formed between them, he knew that Cottus would shoot. Of course he would. It was shoot or risk finding out what this new warrior's sword could do.

With his shield raised, Sebastian just waited for Cottus to really see what Cuchulainn was capable of doing. The pulse blast drained the ambient light from the area, and dimmed to a blip before it even reached the shield. Idris hadn't been kidding, Sebastian thought. Pulse dampening technology was difficult to make mobile. It was in use around the cities, an especially important addition to the defenses in case an artillery mech was in play and happened to miss.

Sebastian grinned to himself. "My turn."

He charged at Cottus, shield still up, still draining the effectiveness of Cottus's blasts as the giant tried to find a weak spot in technology specifically designed to stop long-range barrages. The giant moved at the last second, and while Sebastian would have liked a direct hit on the brute's torso, his blade still found a home. With a sizzling slash, he severed several arms and fingers from Cottus's right-hand side, including that which held the pulse cannon.

The giant screamed, more out of rage than pain, and swung its left arms limply towards Cuchulainn. Sebastian was spun through the air by the force of the impact, landing with a thud that shook through the cockpit and dropping his sword.

"Sebastian, are you alright?" Idris asked.

"He's a tough one," Sebastian replied. "But so am I." Cuchulainn righted itself, and Sebastian loosened up. "Okay, let's try that again." He reached to his back, and withdrew the spear that Idris had told him would be placed there. It extended to its full length, longer than Cuchulainn was tall and shimmering with ionised energy running throughout.

"Your sword is near Cottus. He won't know how to make it work, but he can still hit you with it if he gets a hand on it," Idris told him.

"Dare I ask how you know that?" He didn't need an answer. Looking past Cottus, he could see a Flaran shuttle making its way towards the battlefield. The pulse of Adam's mind reached Sebastian as he stared at the ship. "What are you two doing out here?"

"Helping," Idris said firmly. "We've got one chance at this. You think you can handle it? Adam will help you time it."

He felt the Flaran's mind pulsing against his own, and a smile crept onto his face.

Cuchulainn began its race towards Cottus, while the Flaran shuttle approached from the other side. The giant was visibly divided, unsure which of its enemies it wanted to kill first, the metal soldier or the target that had escaped its grasp a decade ago.

Its hesitation was all they needed. With a nudge from Adam, Sebastian sent Cuchulainn's spear soaring through the air towards Cottus. At the same time, the Flaran sent a telepathic blast at Cottus. Adam already knew from experience that the Baxoon couldn't be stopped completely by a single Flaran, but the distraction was all they needed.

Cuchulainn's spear embedded itself in Cottus's chest, and pinned him in place when the energy inside erupted through his nervous system.

Still, Sebastian kept up his run, scooping up his sword as he closed the gap. He thought of Raquel's sacrifice, to allow them to fight another day. He thought of his father, wishing his soldier son would provide him a grandchild; a future would have to do, Sebastian thought. He thought of Emma and her infinite patience for Ernest Wells. He thought of Adam and the other Flaran who had arrived on Earth a decade ago. And he thought of Idris, the man who grounded him and gave him strength, the man who made the future worth fighting for, and the past worth suffering through. The man he loved, and who loved him back. The man he wouldn't just die for, but the man he would let himself live for.

The sword cut cleanly, burning air and flesh and bone, and when Cottus's head crashed to the ground, the battle was won. Nothing else the Baxoon could throw at them that day could match the tyrant with a hundred hands.

"So what now?" Idris asked.

They stood in the hanger, under the shadow of Cuchulainn. Augustus and Claudius stood to each side of the glistening mech. The remains of Geryon were laid out across the hanger, where teams were working to figure out how to put it all back together.

Haller and Pesce were toasting to Leclert, crying in the shadows and into their drinks.

Adam had returned to the other Flaran, to rejoice in the news that Cottus had been slain at last. They were still trapped on Earth, forced to make it their home a long time ago, but the monster that had plagued their nightmares was gone.

"Now, we get married," Sebastian told him. "We live, and we fight, and we survive, and we live a little bit more. And hopefully someone can work out how the Baxoon masked their recent arrivals. Maybe we can learn how to close the breach they've been travelling through."

"Let's not get ahead of ourselves," Idris remarked.

"Right, right." Sebastian took Idris's hand. "We'll start with this. With us."

"And then?"

Sebastian smiled. "Well, my dad's always saying he wants a grandkid?"

Idris kissed him on the cheek. "I think we can work on that."

CORE DREAMS – QUINN CLANCY

The first day of a new job is always tough. The first day of the job you've been working toward all your life? Terrifying, with a dash of excitement. Putting on the light blue shirt and navy pants that constituted the Garda uniform was a dream come true. The shirt was crisp and tight across my shoulders and the pants crease was sharp enough to shave with. A quick look in the mirror showed a nervous young man, pale skin with a crew cut strawberry blonde hair. No — I stood up straighter and held my head high — a new Garda.

It gave me the confidence I needed to suppress the terror and focus on the excitement of a new job. I gathered a cup of tea to go, shoved toast into me gob and locked up. One of my new neighbours was coming back into their house with a basket under her arm. The young couple had moved in next door over 6 months ago. I'd had to go through training in Templemore and hadn't gotten a chance to get to know them yet. From what I'd seen since coming back, they seemed to have settled in nicely.

My parents had bought an old farmhouse beside a bungalow the original owners had built for their later years. We were each other's only neighbours for miles around. The original owner stayed in that bungalow until passing only last year. The couple moved in shortly after. They seemed to really embrace country living, starting their own coop with several chickens, though I didn't appreciate their rooster waking me most mornings since I'd returned. I raised my hand holding my keys as a hello and got into the car.

I headed towards the Dublin border crossing. If there was any disappointment in finally succeeding in my years long dream, it was getting assigned to a station in the Pale. I'd hoped to remain in the countryside where I felt more help was needed, Though I suppose with Dublin housing 1.5 million people it probably needed all the gardaí it could get. Even with all the sarchumachtaí patrolling. And those superheroes only protected the cities.

Like every kid in the world I'd dreamed to be part of the less than half a percent of people who would develop superpowers, rising to the elite title of sarchumachtaí and like nearly all of them was disappointed when I didn't. My parents used to take me and my sister into the Pale to see the sarchumachtaí headquarters on O'Connell street, where we'd wait for a glimpse of those masked heroes.

When my family was shot down in one of the many terrorist attacks over reunifying Ireland it was a garda who helped them and later me. It was what confirmed my desire to help those outside the barricaded cities. And now I was working in one. Oh well I'm sure once I'd completed my year's probation I could transfer out of the Pale to where I could do the most good.

Pulling up to one of the Dublin border guard's booths where it seemed my other new neighbour worked. I recognised him once he came out of the booth to begin examining the car for weapons. Crap, what was his name again, Chris? Charles? Cathal? I could only remember that it began with a 'C'.

He started the border check with a physical review of the vehicle, even ducking down to flash a light at the undercarriage. Next was a knock on the boot, which I opened. While he went about his duty - preventing terrorists from blowing up Dublin like they had in the late eighties - I kept straining to see his name badge, after all it was just there. Yet it always seemed that bit too far away.

Finally, my neighbour came around to my window and I let it down. Now that it was closer, I could see the brass nameplate showing 'Michael'. So much for his name starting with a 'C'.

"Oh, hey. Tadhg wasn't it?" Michael asked. "Fancy seeing you here. Sorry to pry but the job insists I ask the purpose of your visit to Dublin."

"No worries, Michael. I'm on my way to the new job. Garda at Pearse station. Here's my ID." I smiled while handing over my driver's license. It felt so good to say I was a garda releasing the last of my terror.

"Congrats." Michael took my license and noted me down on his clipboard. "Guess we'll be seeing lots of each other then? Unless you're going to move into the Pale?"

I took my license back with a laugh. "No plans to move, ever. I love where we are."

"Yeah, Margie adores having the chickens to look after and the peace of the area. Well everything's clear here so good luck and see you later." Michael gave a nod and started walking towards his hut.

A glance at the clock showed me running about 15 minutes late, so I made a mental note to leave earlier in future. Clearly the border crossing was going to take more time than I'd anticipated. I sped off as fast as I could to Pearse Street.

Since my new station was right in the city centre, beside Trinity College, parking was at a premium. I spotted several cars double parked in front of the station. Luck must have been shining on me as I was able to sneak into a spot right at the curb beside the granite faced building. It towered over me with a slight curve as it got to the junction. The triple arches that marked the main entrance held carved busts of former officers and a traditional blue lamp above the doors themselves. I liked to believe the busts were some of the first gardaí that were in this building.

I entered through the solid wooden door into the brightly painted foyer. Ahead was another set of double doors, with frosted glass surrounding it and a number pad beside it. To the right a series of benches and pamphlets facing the large mahogany desk built out of the wall to my left. There was no way to get behind the desk without going through the building, as seen by the door behind it. Manning the desk was a portly white man in the garda uniform. He looked to be in his forties with salt and pepper hair and bushy beard.

"You a new probie? You're one of the last ones to arrive." He looked up at a clock and tutted. "Cutting it a bit tight, huh? Better head in."

He pushed something I couldn't see and the door in front of me buzzed. Inside was less welcoming. Industrial green walls and grey tiles reflecting the fluorescent light greeted me. If I didn't know it was a building I'd think I was at the start of a maze of corridors. The only decent part of the construction was the fact that they were wide. I wondered which of the three directions before me I should head in, when the guy on desk came from my left.

"Let's get you to the main bullpen. Paul, by the way." He started down straight leaving me to follow.

"Tadhg. Nice to meet you."

"Culchie?" I nodded and he sighed. "Swear they send us all the fresh ones to knock corners off. Well we've big Tadhg, and small Tadhg. You'll have to find something else."

"What about Tag?" I asked, unsure if names were that important right now. We were passing so many closed doors along the corridor and I had no idea what was behind each. I would get a tour of the building, right?

"Tag. Yeah it'll work."

We walked until we reached a closed door. He opened it and we walked into a wall of noise. Phones ringing, voices chatting and people pounding on keyboards. The captain was already crossing towards the top of the room before he noticed us entering. He was white with short grey hair slicked back and with a side part. Even if I hadn't learnt how to recognise his stripes I'd have pegged him as the man in charge by his confident walk. He made a beeline towards us, his head scanning the various desks in the room.

He'd almost reached us when he called out. "Grace? Grace, get your ass over here."

A smart looking garda stood up, her hair cut into a shiny bob. "Captain?"

"Looks like your probie got here. Tadhg right?"

I nodded but Paul beside me piped up. "He's already said we can call him Tag. Got enough Tadhg's around here."

The Captain's face flashed impatience before smoothing over. "Thanks Paul, so glad to have the names sorted out. Go get settled. I'll start the briefing in a minute." He turned to myself and Grace making it clear Paul wasn't part of this conversation. "You two are together. Grace will show the ropes around here. You'll find we're busier than you thought, even for the city.."

He walked away and straight to the far side of the room opposite the big windows. The walls were covered in various notices and flyers, a large rota, and two doors. The Captain went right to the centre where a number of mug shots were pinned. Most I didn't recognise, however the few criminal sarchumachtaí were obvious.

Grace gave a small chuckle. "You'll get used to his brusque attitude. Captain O'Leary will have your back as much as he can so don't worry if he doesn't talk your ear off."

"Thanks." I gave her a strained smile, my anxiety rising now I knew who I needed to impress to keep my job.

I went to say more but the captain started talking at the top of the room. Except for a few who were on the phone, the cacophony in the room dimmed for his voice to be heard without shouting.

"Alright, people, let's get this rolling. Welcome all the new members of the force, you'll find this district tough but the people beside you will support and protect you. You've all met your partners and they'll show you what the job is really about.

"Now, aside from standard routes we've had several incidents of mugging in Stephen's Green so I want an extra patrol out there. We're still going through the evidence from the attempted robbery the Warden stopped yesterday. Unfortunately somebody has to go interview the Warden so one of the new teams gets that joy. Don't worry, you'll all get a chance to work with Warden.

"Check your assignments and stay safe out there." With a sharp nod, the captain walked out of the room as the buzz started intensifying again.

"Okay, newbie, we're going out on patrol. Let's get kitted up." Grace led me out of the bullpen. She was slower walking through the building pointing out storerooms, records, interrogation rooms. Soon we reached the locker room with all the necessary equipment.

Grace directed me to a fresh locker beside hers and we got started pulling on our full kit, including stab vests, a vest with more pockets than necessary, and the fluorescent jacket in that order. "Hey Grace, what did the Captain mean about working with the Warden?"

Grace raised an elegant eyebrow. "Didn't you know about how he's based in this station? You'll hear lots about him. From him, too. Actually, getting him to shut up is the biggest problem."

"We have a sarchumachta in-house?" It felt like my brain

stuttered to a stop. It was well known they all worked out of their own headquarters. They occupied the old Savoy hotel on O'Connell street where they could all be seen.

"We're one of the busiest districts in the country, so the higher ups decided we could do with one. I see him in his office more than out there though." Grace rolled her eyes, double checking the fastenings of everything. "Just wait, we'll end up arresting someone today.

"In-house sarchumachaí wasn't covered in Templemore."

"Yeah, you're in the real world now."

We didn't make an arrest that day but it was busy and filled with minor issues. In fact my whole first week was filled with drunk students, lost tourists, and complaints. So many complaints. And every hour seemed to fill up faster than I wanted. It was my second week before I encountered a sarchumachta fight.

One of the few villainous sarchumachta, Rosie, decided to rob Brown Thomas. Several heroes including ours got involved in the fight, and one of the massive display windows got destroyed. I was called in at the end, my patrol apparently more important than people in trouble. Once there we got assigned to watch that window.

I'm not going to lie, it was boring. Just standing there and making sure nobody else tried to rob the place. What was worse was the obnoxious teens hurling verbal abuse our way. My blood boiled and it took everything I had to stay still and keep asking them to move along. Eventually one spat at us, and Grace immediately handcuffed him. I thought I'd feel relief at that, maybe get in and do some paperwork. Instead, when she called it in, a patrol car came down and met us at the bottom of Grafton Street and carried the punk away.

We were stuck back babysitting a building after that.

I met the Warden not long after that. We came back to the station tired and sore from a long day of just standing. The Warden sat in the middle of the bullpen like king of the castle. He was too busy regaling his 'glorious' battle to notice that nobody was really paying attention.

I followed Grace's lead in slinking to my desk and trying not to look at him.

"Well if it isn't one of the probies. Get there for my big fight?" Warden wandered over to me, his fluorescent yellow and grey outfit a riot of colours in the busy blue office. Come to think of it, I'd not seen any sarchumachtaí wearing a normal outfit or muted colours. Even Rosie supposedly wore a skin tight lavender catsuit and leather jacket. The Warden's light grey jeans were striped with yellow, his armoured vest continued that colour scheme with yellow highlights, and even his domino mask was yellow.

I shook my head. "Sorry, I only got called in at the end. Congratulations on the arrest."

"Oh, we didn't arrest Rosie. The slippery eel got away. Next time, though," he waved a hand as though leaving a powerful criminal on the loose wasn't a major problem. He settled his large frame onto a chair beside me. "You missed the best parts of the fight.

"There Rosie was, holding some rich woman hostage, as her minions were holding up cashiers demanding money. The first thing I did was raise barriers on the guns so if the minions tried to fire, the guns would explode. Better to have fewer criminals, am I right? Well, they've obviously heard of what I can do so they all dropped those guns and took out knives.

"There were at least seven between me and Rosie. Oh, and her hostage, she was shrieking so much it would have been hard to focus for any other sarchumachtaí. But not me, I dashed in, shielding my arm and *bam*! Straight into the first guy's face, broken nose and down he went. The next guy must have decided I was too strong for him because he ran away. Instead the next two tag-teamed me. We were exchanging blows, but of course they didn't have my training so they were sloppy. I, of course, was lulling them into a false sense of security, letting them tire.

"Course, there's no honour amongst thieves, and two more joined the fray. I decided to stop playing with them and gave them my trademarked shield slam, knocking them all out on the floor. Next -" At some point I tuned him out and went back to work.

The words in my report had started blurring when it hit quitting time. Grace knocked on the desk beside me. "Hey, you want to grab a pint before heading home?"

"I'd like to, but I'm living outside the Pale, might be a long trip later out the Lucan gate," I hedged. Not that I didn't want to spend some time and ask Grace questions about the force that might be best said outside these walls.

"Perfect, my favourite bar is near the border crossing there. Sounds like a good halfway point between us."

"Sure, sounds good."

We both carefully put away the official kit in our lockers, before heading out. I followed her car to the pub. It had a good atmosphere without being rowdy. A quick look around showed it a favourite of more than a few gardaí. At least, it looked that way as so many of the patrons had their backs to the wall.

I got the first round, just a shandy for myself, and settled into the chair opposite hers. It had a good view of the back door, while she got to watch the front. She played a little with coasters in front of her before speaking. "So, managed your first two weeks on the job. How you finding it?"

"Busier than I anticipated, but the work itself is more boring than training made it out to be."

"Don't get too complacent. The sarchumachtaí are being quiet for some reason. We deal with their fallout more often than not."

"About that, is Warden always that … pompous?" I asked carefully.

I needn't have bothered. Grace snorted and smiled at me. "If anything he was extra egotistical today with some fresh blood to entertain. He'll grow bored eventually."

"Is he really that unconcerned with letting Rosie go?" I asked the question that had bothered me all day. "She's killed a ton of people."

"I thought you figured out that the sarchumahtaí are all out for attention and praise. Wouldn't surprise me if the people who have powers get indoctrinated into that life." Grace shook her head. "As much as I hate working with the Warden, I think if we got all of them attached to a garda station they might do more good."

"They're certainly needed in the countryside." Memories swelled of that particular terrorist attack where I lost everything, stopping me from continuing.

Grace studied my face before nodding her head. "Nobody's going to come and save this little island, we need to stand up and do it ourselves." She held out her pint glass.

"I'm with you on that." I tapped it with mine. A promise as much as a toast.

It was late when I passed through border control and was surprised to see Michael there. I waited for him to do his checks and rolled down the window.

"Working late aren't you?" I asked.

"Yeah, one of the crew called in sick so I got volun-told to take the shift. I'm taking half and somebody from tomorrow gets to start early." He frowned, clearly unhappy with the situation.

"Dang, that sucks." I could commiserate. I'd had to work some overtime already but not that much.

"You're late enough aren't you? Working the Rosie robbery?"

It didn't surprise me that he'd heard about it already. The radio stations kept talking about the 'epic fight' between our heroes and the 'evil' Rosie. Not that she wasn't a murderous psychopath, but it sounded like they got all their information straight from the Warden himself.

"Not senior enough for that, just guarded the building. Went out with my partner for a pint after."

"Oh man, I haven't gotten out for a pint in a while. That is one thing I miss out here." A look of longing passed his face.

"You should join us sometime," I offered without thinking. It would be nice to chat to somebody I hadn't spent all day with.

"You sure your partner won't mind that?" I could see the hope on his face.

"Yeah, she's sound out. I think as long as you're not going to sit talking about all your accomplishments you're more than welcome."

"Yeah, like I've so much to be proud of taking down reg plates and driver's licenses." Michael shook his head and chuckled.

"See, you'll fit in perfectly. It's as exciting as our job."

The rest of my first month flew by, it was a real highlight being greeted by Michael on the way into the city and out on the times our schedules matched.

Before I knew it, it was my first day of giving court testimony. I was glad that it brought back that nervous bubbling in my stomach. Nothing about this job was what I thought it was. I met a bored looking Grace at the top of the stairs, her uniform perfect as always.

"Ready for a long day, Tag?" She sipped from her travel mug.

"We're only here for the morning, I'm sure it won't be that bad." I gave her a smile that didn't seem to land as she just looked at me like I didn't know what I was talking about. To be fair, she had been to more of these than me.

"Whatever you say, newbie."

She led me into the small court building. The fancy new one seemed to be mostly for higher profile cases - for the sarchumachta - not small drug charges.

I was so conditioned to US television and movies the actual courtroom surprised me. It looked more like a small church than a courtroom. There wasn't any jury box, and the benches behind were more like pews. The walls were painted cream, and light streamed in from the two windows setting off the wood in the furniture.

Grace got me settled near the back of the benches and we watched as cases passed by us. I was shocked by how many people got warnings, or light fines. I wasn't expecting massive amounts of jail time but I'd thought there'd be at least some. Then our perp came up and I gave my testimony on his crime as best I could, giving off a confidence I didn't feel. I made sure to emphasise that the perp would reoffend and be dealing the minute he left.

But he got off.

I somehow managed to keep a calm demeanour until we were back in the car. Then I exploded. "What the hell just happened?"

"Justice in Ireland." Grace took the lid of her cup and peered in.

"That's not right." I banged the steering wheel for emphasis.

"No, but it's what we have." Dissatisfied to see it empty, she placed the mug in the passenger well. "I wish I could change it, but there's nothing we can do."

"What can we do?" Part of me felt ripped open. After the long hours, harassment, and even assaults this couldn't be all there was.

"Our jobs." For the first time, the thought depressed me.

I'd only just started the third shift when we got called out to a domestic disturbance. When we pulled up to the building, I could hear the couple screaming at each other as I got out. All my training told me this was going to be a hard call and my barely formed instincts agreed with that sentiment.

We walked over to the door and hit the buzzer. A minute passed and there was no response. Grace tried one more time with no success and went for a neighbour.

"Hello?" A feminine voice came out fuzzy from the intercom.

"Garda Síochána, we're here about a domestic disturbance?" Grace replied.

"Oh thank goodness. They've been at it an hour, and it's just getting worse. Come in." The sound of buzzing was barely heard and I pulled open the door into dingy stairs. The screaming got louder as we walked up two flights to the apartment. Grace nodded at me and I rapped hard on the door.

The door opened revealing a broad man in a grey tracksuit with a white tee shirt and belly spilling out. He looked like everybody else. I'd have passed him in the street and waved or nodded a greeting. Just a man at the end of the work day, maybe a little ruddy from some drink but no different from Michael. Well, Michael kept himself better than this guy.

"What do you pigs want?" The man sneered at us.

"We've been called out because of a potential domestic disturbance, is everything okay?" Grace took the lead.

"Domestic disturbance? Nosy bloody neighbours. Everything's

fine. Just a normal argument." The man seemed to roll his eyes at us.

"May we see your partner please?" Grace asked.

"It's ten o'clock at night, bugger off. Everybody is fine." His lips curled even as his face got redder.

"I'm sorry sir, but we need to hear that from her." Grace held firm, keeping her voice the same steady tone.

"Stop being so stubborn, Henry, just let them in." The woman shouted.

"Can you come to the door, please, ma'am?" Grace called back.

"Look, you've heard from her she's fine, go away." Henry went to slam the door but found my foot blocking it. I was glad to have my steel-toed boots on as the impact still stung.

"Sir, please let us into the apartment and speak to your partner for a minute." Grace's tone turned colder and I really hoped the man would just listen and let us get on with it. Honestly, unlike some of the more horrifying calls I'd had since I'd started, this seemed less severe. They probably argued all the time and didn't get any further than that. Annoying for their neighbours but not endangering either person.

"I know my rights! You can't just barge in here. Go away." Henry came out from behind the door and took a swing at Grace. I had a moment of regret for what I had just been thinking, before reacting and wrestling Henry away from her. He struggled and had a fierce elbow but thankfully I subdued him quickly and got him locked up in my handcuffs.

Once Grace was sure I had everything in hand, she opened the door into the cramped flat. The room was maybe ten feet wide by twenty feet long. A ratty brown couch sat against the wall to the left before a door. The kitchen area was a few counters at the back of the room and the detritus of life littered on the floor. A pile of dirty dishes was stacked on the counter beside where the woman stood. Bleach blonde in a pair of velour tracksuit bottoms and a string tank top.

Her eyes widened as Grace entered the apartment and then she got a glimpse of me coming in behind with the handcuffed Henry.

"Hey, you leave my Henry alone, he's not doing anything wrong," the woman shrieked. She grabbed a knife from the counter and started swinging it at Grace.

I tugged Grace forward in time to see the blade flash past her. Grace managed to spin around and catch the woman's arm before she could make another strike. She grabbed the woman's wrist and twisted it like we were shown in Templemore.

The knife clattered to the floor and the woman started cussing us black and blue.

"Dee? Dee? Are you okay? Don't you hurt her, you mother-" I pulled him away from the apartment before he could finish his epithet. Seems love wasn't dead. Just loud.

I sighed and brought the belligerent Henry down the stairs and into the car. I radioed in to get another squad car in to collect his partner.

I waited impatiently until the second car arrived and watched as the new garda went up to the apartment. Grace came down not long after, followed by the woman struggling in the grasp of my colleagues.

It wasn't until we got back to the station and had locked up our domestics that I noticed the knife had managed to slice some of her shoulder. She was obstinate and didn't want it looked at but I managed to talk her into it. It turned out to be a minor injury that only needed some antiseptic and a bandage. We were back on patrol within half an hour.

The rest of the night was a lot calmer, if you can say a bunch of rowdy drunks can be quiet. At least, it was until we reached the end of our shift and Captain O'Leary asked us to see him.

Henry and Dee wanted to press charges for police brutality, and trespassing. We were getting a day's holiday while everything was checked out. Unpaid naturally.

Something must have broken in me that night. The days passed in a haze as I got up, had my tea, and left for the station. I think Mike must have picked up on it, because he barely made an effort to chat as I travelled through anymore. No, that was saved for the rare occasions he came out to get a pint with Grace and myself.

It was a couple of months before he said something that caught my attention and helped brighten the world. "Margie is pregnant! We're going to have a baby."

"Congratulations. I know you've been wanting this for a while." I clapped him on the shoulder while Grace raised her pint.

"Yeah, it's been so hard not saying anything to you since we found out. Only passed the first trimester last week."

I bought a round of drinks and contemplated the simple joys of life. Maybe I needed to get out dating.

Court days were a blur of the same thing. I met a bored-looking Grace at the top of the stairs.

"Ready for a long day, Tag?" She sipped from her travel mug.

At this point I nodded agreement and shared a pastry with her. It was the only sweet thing about today.

The inside hadn't changed but it should have looked better. Less grey. Less dingy. I wasn't sure if the shine was off the wood or me.

We settled near the back of the benches and we watched as cases passed by us. Warning. Warning. Fine. Oh, that one got a couple of years in jail. Never mind, a suspended sentence. Warning. Then our drug dealer came up and I gave my testimony as best I could, giving off a confidence I didn't feel. I made sure to emphasise that the perp would reoffend and be dealing the minute he left.

But he got off.

We were on patrol and the sun was splitting the sky. The bulky uniform and accoutrements felt much heavier than they should have. I was glad for every little breeze I could get as Grace and I walked around Temple Bar. The crowded streets didn't allow for fast movement, but everybody was having a good time. The night crowds and really rowdy drunks hadn't appeared yet. In many ways it was one of the best days on the job so far.

Funny how nice it was to have the hardest question I had to answer being the location of a Dublin landmark that I had no clue of. Grace was either more in touch with Dublin life or had been asked enough times to know the answer.

The first sign of trouble was a booming clang. It was so out of place there was a silence as everybody tried to locate the issue. A nearby wall sprouted smoke and dust.

From it a form fell nearly crashing to the ground but righted itself. I was frozen in shock as Rosie emerged from the cloud. Her form fitting black leather pants with a silver and black biker jacket lost some of their intimidation from the fine layer of dust covering it.

My brain felt like it was in a complete shut down. A wanted criminal was in front of me so I should do something. But Rosie had the ability to call on the earth. Not something I could easily prevent.

And there behind her was a large indent in the wall. How did that get in there. Then it clicked. A sarchumactha fight.

Grace twigged it quicker and pulled out her radio. She started calling for backup and for the Warden to get out here. She then grabbed on my sleeve and directed me to start escorting the people out of the area. Not that they hadn't gotten the idea already if the instant screaming wasn't a suggestion.

I moved fast and started implementing the crowd control tactics we were taught at Temple Mor. Faces blurred past me, as did dust. I did my best to ignore the sounds of a fight behind me and just on the people around us.

When I saw another navy and fluorescent uniform that wasn't Grace, I felt a sigh of relief. Especially when they were followed up by more. Within a few blinks the crowd shifted from helpless bystanders to the Gardaí. Taking a chance to look at the fight, my eye almost glossed over the grey and yellow of the Warden. He was far out from the fight, only barely closer than the gardaí. Instead it was a Chulainn, one who's powers was mostly strength based, trying to pummel Rosie.

Rosie had used the earth on her catsuit as portable armour, visible by its cobblestone texture similar to that under her feet. I could just make out the shimmer of Warden's shields going into place behind her, and sliding forward like trying to sweep a spider up onto a sheet of paper. I was very confused.

Was he trying to separate her from the ground? Would that stop her from using her powers? We'd not gotten into how the powers of sarchumachtaí worked in training.

It seemed mute anyway as Chulainn successfully feinted left before landing a hard right to Rosie's chin and knocked her out. When I checked later it turned out the whole thing happened in about five minutes total. Silence descended interrupted by the squawk of radio's. Dust and dirt settled in the surround and Chulainn was watching Rosie's fallen form to ensure she wasn't faking.

"Another epic battle, eh, Cú?" Warden's voice echoed in the silence and movement started happening. Chulainn took a strong plastic tie to handcuff Rosie, while the Warden filled the scene the way he didn't during the fight.

It was a signal to everybody else as the orders soon got handed out and some of the gardaí that showed up to support started dispersing, even as others started cordoning off the area to make the crime scene easier to process.

I helped out as Chulainn gathered up Rosie in a fireman's sling and started walking away with the Warden still prattling beside him. Grace and I were soon pulled to give our statements about the start of the incident. We had just started when there was a frenzy of activity near the cratered wall Rosie smashed into. Somebody had found a body, crushed by the detritus of the fight. Another tally to Rosie's death count, just somebody out to shop the city centre, and killed for no good reason. My heart felt heavy as we recounted the last minutes of their life.

When we returned to Pearse Street the Warden was already regaling the room of the 'thrilling' battle that sounded vastly different from what I watched.

The only comfort was nobody was listening to him.

Mike was pale when he entered the pub and I knew something was up. "Hey Mike!" I called over.

He came towards us, lacking any real purpose. He sat down and stared at the table in front of him.

"Mike? Is everything okay? It's not Margie is it?" Grace asked, reaching a hand out to him.

He shook his head before letting out a ragged breath. I got up and grabbed a round, carefully putting his pint in front of him. He immediately gripped it so hard I thought the glass would shatter.

"Did a routine stop like always. Was friendly with the guy, he's a carpenter, does nixers in the Pale every now and then. He had lots of wood in the back of the van. But also explosives. My superiors are telling me, there was enough C4 in there to blow up most of the border crossing."

Grace sucked in a deep breath and I widened my eyes. That was a huge thing to stop. No wonder he looked so pale.

"I think rounds are on us tonight. You drink up and forget it." Grace raised her class as if to toast. We followed suit if a bit confused. "To another day."

The glasses clinked, but there wasn't much cheer to be had.

The day slunk in grey and with that awful misty rain. Court day again.

We settled in what had become our usual places and we watched as cases passed by us. Though I don't know why when the results never changed. Then our case where I gave my testimony as best I could, faking a confidence I didn't feel. I tried a new tactic when discussing how the perp would reoffend.

But he got off.

The months blurred again. Not even the supposedly 'epic' fight between the Warden in our station and one of the terrorist captains registered more than boredom with me. 53 people died that day, but aside from a brief mention in the paper of the deaths, nobody was talking about them. It was all how wonderful the Warden was. How so much of the city would have been lost without him. It all sickened me. It became so hard not to want to punch him.

It was late when I got in and I just didn't want to do anything. My bones felt tired and once I sat down on the couch I didn't have the energy to get back up and get some dinner. I decided to wait until my stomach complained louder than my bones. The sun was setting and not even the darkened room could make me get up. What finally got me out of the near vegetable state I was in though, was my phone.

It rang loudly with the ringtone for Margie. Groaning I got up and answered it. "Mar-"

"Tag, somebody's trying to break in. Mike's on duty, you have to come help." Margie hissed down the line.

A sudden flash of worry crossed me, before the weight of tiredness slammed through me dragging me down and drowning out any concern. "I'm out of jurisdiction, Margie. Get into a closet and call 911. I'll ring them, too."

"Can you come over, please?" Her voice was shaky.

"Sorry." I hung up and plopped into the chair beside the table I'd left my phone on. I was too weary to help really. I'd get fresh gardaí out here who could help, I rang the switch and laid out what Margie had told me.

"Okay, Officer, we've notified your local station and they're sending out patrol cars now to investigate. Stay inside and stay safe." The calm feminine voice told me.

"Shouldn't I at least go over and help?" My conscience was starting to nag me.

"You're not in your district. Stay inside and stay safe." They repeated, confirming I'd made the right choice.

I signed off with assurances and just stared. This chair faced the shadowed room, a glint of the outside light reflecting off the mirror I hadn't looked at once. My mother's handmade blanket seemed haloed in the dual streams of light. My own mother, who was shot down by terrorist crossfire with my dad and little sister. I wasn't the only person outside the Pale with that sob story. Rural Ireland was the battleground for independence and no sarchumachta was going to

Screw this. Helping people like Margie, helping my neighbours, that was the real reason I wore the stinking uniform. I wasn't going to sit here and let them get hurt when I had the power to do something.

I pushed up, reinvigorated. I took a moment to pick up my old hurl and the spare set of keys I had for them. I'd not used the hurl for years but the memories of playing with my father made me keep it. Right now, I was thinking it was a long solid wooden stick that I was familiar with. I wasn't going to let another tragedy happen and just stand by.

I grabbed the spare key Margie and Mike had given me for their house. I considered whether to use their front or back door, eventually deciding to go via the back. So I slipped out the back door and made my way over to the fence. I was glad to have had the wooden panels replaced recently as it meant I was able to boost myself over silently. By pure luck the idiot whom I landed behind didn't notice me, but he felt it when I cracked him over the head with my hurl. Well, maybe less luck, and more the angry sound of alarmed chickens.

The crack got the attention of the intruder currently mucking about with the back door lock. He spun around and raised his arm. I threw myself to the left and rolled, coming up to land another swing of the hurl on his outstretched arm. He cried out in pain and I gave him a whack over the head too, just to make sure he would be out of this fight.

I quickly unlocked the door and entered. I slammed the door shut and locked it again. I left the keys there as a preventative from lock picking. Pain bloomed on the left side of my face as a can of beans dropped to the floor. I spun over, hurl at the ready, to see Margie limned in the light from the window. She held another can and looked ready to throw it again.

"It's me!" I hissed at her and came over to grab her arm before she could throw anything else my way.

"I thought you couldn't come." Her eyes glistened but her voice was steady.

"Yeah, I was given strict orders not to be here.

"So why are you?" her sniffle reduced the harshness of her accusation.

"Because I joined the gardaí to help people, and it's not working if I can't even help my neighbours. So I'm defying orders and got my butt over here.

She gave a half sob, half laugh. "I'm glad you did."

I wrapped an arm around her for a minute. "Right, my original orders to find a closet to hide in remain. You need to be safe. For you and the little one."

"Do you really think this thing will fit in a wardrobe?" Margie motioned to her admittedly large baby bump.

"I don't know, but it's the safest place I can think of right now. Go." I pushed her towards the stairs and she stumbled a bit but found her legs quickly and raced up the stairs. Waddled was more accurate, but it was the fastest waddle I'd ever seen.

I walked forward to the hall, and pushed the door open a jar.

There were obviously lights on in the sitting room to the left of the front door. The door itself didn't show much beyond some shadows moving that could be trees or something else. I doubted the two I'd encountered were the only ones attacking.

The time stretched out to an eternity while I stood and watched that door. I'm not sure how long passed when I got my first whiff of it. Diesel. Strong enough I felt like I was near a petrol station. I cursed again, after all I'd told Margie to go upstairs thinking the danger was physical, not a fire.

I lost another moment considering rushing outside to confront the attackers or going upstairs to get Margie out. Visions of gunfire stopped my rush and I thundered up the stairs.

"Margie!" I shouted, not caring if they heard us outside or not.

A sound came from the nursery and I pulled open the wardrobe to find Margie clutching a metal hanger. The kind you could bend with one hand. She may have a fighting spirit but no weapon sense. "Are they gone?"

"No, I think they're setting a fire. We have to go." I took her arm and started leading her away.

"What? No, what about the nursery? We've just got it right." I felt her resisting my attempts to drag her away but not for long as she followed me down.

"Let's worry about the baby for the nursery first." I was so glad to have left the key in the lock as it saved some time allowing me to fling it open. Neither person had moved in the time I was in the house, and I had a passing wish that I hadn't killed them.

"Where can we go? Oh no, we have to release the chickens!"

"They're far enough from the house they'll be fine, Margie. And we'll head over to my house. Maybe we can get to the car and drive away from here."

"But they'll see us."

"Not over the fence."

She gave it a wary look, but allowed me to boost her over. Or at least on the top. Once she was secure, I jumped it myself and landed to help her down.

Getting round the house and out the gate was a little like trekking through the jungle because I'd let so many weeds grow. Fortunately, I think it also covered up our escape. I peeked out the side gate and couldn't see anybody. The car was just there, ready for us.

Margie was still struggling with her seatbelt when I peeled out of my driveway. I heard shouts behind me but didn't care. Of course, by the time I reached the end of the road blue and red lights greeted me. The cavalry was late. But at least it showed up.

Captain O'Leary must have seen something on my face when we finished up with the Internal Affairs idiots as he asked me to stay back in his office for a few minutes. I was still on suspension, but O'Leary talked my record up and vouched that having someone willing to help others was a good trait to have in An Garda Síochána. Enough that I would be able to stay in once my suspension was over. I just wasn't sure the force was where I wanted to be any more.

Especially after being lectured about taking on terrorists out for revenge on the guy who stopped one of theirs killing hundreds in a bomb and how I should have left a pregnant woman alone to die. Okay so they didn't use those exact words but there was enough talk about that I could read between the lines. And frankly I was tired of being ineffectual, of focusing on the cities and leaving the countryside to the terrorists. And this meeting just made it clear to me that the sarchumacthaí and the gardaí weren't focused on the terrorists.

There was silence in the office for a minute as the last person left. O'Leary looked tired, dark circles under his eyes highlighted by the stark fluorescent lights.

"We'll be glad to have you back next week, Tag. You and Grace are some of our best officers." He gave me a weary smile.

My thoughts were swirling but one thing was starting to crystalise. "I don't know if I will be back next week. I'm not sure I want to continue being a garda. It seems we don't do enough to help the ordinary person."

O'Leary nodded. "I agree we need to do more, Tadhg, but sometimes all you can do is look out for the community around you. We can only focus on a small area. There isn't enough of us."

"Isn't that the point of the Garda? Look at what's happening in that Meath district. Those terrorists intending to kill a pregnant woman got an apology and are free to hurt others. I can't just sit by and do nothing anymore, not when I can do something. I joined to help those people. Not to get ordered to stay put." I could feel my blood pressure rising as the salient points of that stupid meeting poked at my brain.

"And you are. Here. We might be a small country but we're still too large for one man to save. We need to do it together. Leaving won't solve the problem."

"I'm sorry Captain. I just can't stay. I need to find a better way." I placed my badge on his desk and walked out.

It felt weird getting a beer with Grace after I'd handed in my badge. She'd been so against it I didn't think I'd hear from her again, let alone a day later. The silence was awkward for a moment before she broke it.

"So I've been doing some research and it seems like it's not that hard for garda to become private detectives here in Ireland. Not usual, but not impossible either," Grace said.

"Private detectives? I thought you weren't going to leave the force." I was surprised she'd consider it, especially since she gave such a stink about me leaving.

"Not for me, you." Grace rolled her eyes and it felt like I was brought back to that first day I met her, and she disparaged the need for an in-house sarchumachta. It warmed me knowing that I didn't have all bitter memories from my time.

"What am I going to do with a private detective license?"

"The thing you've always wanted to do. Help people, remind everybody that those outside the cities matter too."

"You think I could make a difference like that?" Part of me was interested, it really hit on what the dream really was.

"Within or without, we'll make a difference." She took a slug of her beer. "Maybe even manage to do it with both."

BETWEEN SHADOWS AND SUNLIGHT – KAT DODD

Nobody knows for sure how the end came or where it started. There were rumours and whispers of government experiments going wrong and subjects escaping before they died. There were other rumours that it wasn't actually a break out but a planned release. But there were always *rumours and whispers and conspiracy theories about the government pulling things like that, this wasn't anything new, and that made it harder to know what was or wasn't the truth.*

Whatever the cause, society did not adapt well or quickly to the zombie apocalypse, and organized civilization collapsed in a very short period as a result. People survived, people adapted, as people always do. Smaller communities than before formed in little pockets. A lot of people opted to be on their own, for various reasons, but even if they didn't trust other people, they would still help when they could. Some went on patrols to rescue anyone they could. Some shared and traded supplies, working together for a short period to get what they needed before going their separate ways again.

Before the end of the world, there was a heartwarming story that would periodically make the rounds on the internet. In it, the morning after a big storm, the beach is covered in starfish stranded on land, and a child is picking starfishes up and throwing them back into the ocean. An old man asks what the child is doing, and laughs when the child explains, and asks the child why do something so futile? The beach is so very big, and there are so very many starfish, what difference could possibly be made? The child picks up another starfish and tosses it back into the water and says they made a difference to that one. In another version, the child says that they'll make more of a difference if the old man helps.

People tend to fall into different categories: people who don't want to help because why should they?, people who want to help but don't know how and get overwhelmed by how insurmountable it seems and where do they even start?, and people who don't care how small or big something is, help is help, and they'll do whatever they can to help whenever they can because why shouldn't *they?, and the last category is the group that's most likely to accomplish things.*

Even after society fell, that remained true. Human nature is frequently one of the most beautiful and most horrific things to be found in the world.

Allie had a routine. She was pretty sure her routine helped keep her alive, so she wasn't really going to change it any time soon. Why fix what wasn't broken, right?

Wake up sometime at the ass crack of dawn, when the birds started screaming at the sun. Undo the straps that she had used to secure herself to whatever tree she'd slept in and pack them up neatly. Everything always got packed up neatly unless she had to *get moving now now now*, but most mornings she could take her time without worrying. Climb down, deal with body functions that couldn't really be done in a tree. Gather plants for breakfast if possible, eat something from her stash if not. Practice drawing her swords cleanly because like hell was she going to die because she'd fumbled it in stress.

(Everyone wanted guns in a zombie apocalypse. Nah. Too loud, and ammo would run out. Sure, you could make your own, but that wasn't usually as good, and while it would do in a pinch, swords were Allie's choice. Allie had swords that she took good care of because they'd been a birthday present before this whole mess even started. She was a bit of an odd duck and she knew that, and her family had known it as well but still encouraged it. But oh boy was that coming in handy now and keeping her alive. So long as she cleaned her swords and kept them sharp they'd last a whole hell of a lot longer than bullets.)

Do morning stretches so that she'd be nice and limber for the day. Brush and braid her hair out of her face. Fiddle with her radio, just on the off chance that maybe this time she'd pick something up, even though she never did. Pick a direction and move on.

She didn't have anywhere she was moving *to*, but it was important to move anyway. Staying still was death.

Allie went through all those steps, singing softly to herself as she did. Sure, noise attracted the roamers, but roamers were slow and Allie was fast. It helped that roamers were *not* a slow, relentless, inevitable death, and were actually very easily distractible, if you could be patient, which Allie wasn't actually good at but was learning how to be.

Unless you got caught between packs of roamers. Then it was just Bad News Bears and you hoped for the best.

But, no, really, the bigger dangers, in Allie's experience, was *people.*

Figured that after the end of the world, humans were still the biggest problem.

Allie stuck to her routine, the same way she always did, otherwise it wouldn't really be a routine. If nothing else, her routine made her feel better and a little more in control.

Hearing someone scream was not part of the routine.

That didn't stop Allie from running towards the scream anyway.

Some people *didn't* try to help. It was easy to get killed trying to help someone, after all. And that was before you got into people trying to take advantage of others or steal their supplies. People aren't always trustworthy, and even Allie knew that.

Allie wasn't fearless by any means. There were a lot of things that she was afraid of. Allie just refused to ever let her fear stop her and she for *damn* sure wouldn't let it keep her from doing the right thing and helping someone who needed it. Allie wouldn't be able to live with herself if she ever didn't do her best and not doing so *may* cost someone their life.

Long before all this mess even started, Allie had decided to help anyone who needed it, rather than ignore the situation. She'd had a lot of times to rethink that, especially in the new world she lived in, but no, that was what she was going to do. She made the same decision every day before she was put in a situation where she'd have to choose quickly what she'd do so that she'd already know.

Because of that decision, it meant that when Allie heard the scream, she was already running towards it before she even really registered what it was. She just tried to run faster, even though she was already running as fast as she could, and ignored the branches and brambles snagging on her clothes and hair and skin. Please just let her get there in time to make a difference. That was all that mattered. She could deal with injuries, she could deal with a lot of things, but she could not deal with failure, not with this.

Allie ran into a clearing, where a young woman about Allie's age was trying to fight a pack of roamers with a stick. She was doing pretty well, all things considered — mostly the consideration being that she wasn't dead yet, since she was fighting with a damn *stick* — but it was just a matter of time until the inevitable happened if she didn't start running. Allie started to wonder why she hadn't already tried to run when Allie realized that the terrified scream hadn't come from the other woman but from the kid behind her.

If Allie *had* been undecided before, which she had *not* been, she absolutely was not now.

You don't abandon kids. Period.

Allie drew her swords smoothly, just the way she'd practiced —

in fact, this was *why* she practiced it as much as she did — running towards the other woman and the child, launching herself between them and the zombies, landing easily.

In her old life, before all this happened, Allie had been a cheerleader. Okay, in her old life, she'd been a lot of things, and cheerleader was only one of those things, but that was the thing she was drawing on now.

"Don't kill them!" The kid's voice was high, indicating stress and fear, but also firm. "You can't kill them."

"Are you-" Allie cut herself off before she called the kid crazy, dodging a clumsy attempt at a bite. "They're not even alive and they're trying to kill *us*," she pointed out, trying to be reasonable.

"Evie doesn't like it," the kid said primly, "so we don't do it. My foot's stuck. Just let Evie get me out of it and we can run. I can run faster than any old zombie."

Allie squared her shoulders and readied herself for more. "I'll keep them distracted and I'll try my best to not kill any of them, but the longer this goes on, the less I can promise that," she finally landed on. She had a weapon, she had the ability to plan, she still had higher brain function, she was strong and she was fast. She had a lot of things in her favour. But zombies were untiring and they wouldn't be stopped by injury. The longer the fight went on, the more the balance would tilt towards them and away from Allie. But truthfully, Allie hated killing if she didn't have to.

She'd been a vegetarian in her old life. Now she didn't have the luxury to stick to that, but she still tried as much as possible. Zombies might be zombies but they'd been human once upon a time, and while Allie knew she was doing what she had to do, that didn't mean she didn't feel bad about it.

"Okie dokie," the kid chirped at her from behind her, and Allie could hear the rustling as Evie tried to extricate the kid from whatever they'd gotten stuck in.

Allie focused, trying to pay attention to all the roamers around her to try to keep any of them from catching her by surprise. Turned out that ADHD came in handy in the apocalypse, which was good since Allie had run out of meds about two weeks after society caught fire. Being able to focus on everything around her was actually a benefit in this new normal, and it was less exhausting to no longer be constantly shutting that down. Any noise Allie heard, she was already reacting to by the time her conscious brain caught up to process whatever it was. She kept hitting with the flat of her sword as much as possible, trying to keep to her end of the bargain with the other two.

"Ready," the kid reported, and Allie could already hear the fall of their footsteps as they started to run.

Allie flipped neatly away to put some distance between herself and the roamers, twisting in the air to land facing the other direction so that she could join Evie and the kid, easily keeping pace with them.

Allie was totally going to have to ask the kid's name. Wasn't like Allie could keep on using "*the kid*", after all.

Okay, Allie *could*, but that didn't mean that she *should*.

"Got anywhere you're running *to* or are you just running *from*?" Allie asked between breaths, measuring her breathing out and timing them to her footfalls so that she wouldn't get out of breath before they'd gotten very far. Allie *hated* running, if she were completely honest, but Allie had learned the basic tricks for running back when one of her brothers was training for marathons. She hadn't paid all that much attention at the time, and she sure wished she had now. She'd just been way more interested when he had taught her how to break into a car and hotwire it, "*just in case*" she ever needed it. Which, hey, she had. So Jordan had been right about that.

"Running from," the kid answered. "But from seems like a good idea? If it keeps us away from the zombies?"

Allie led them down some deer trails and back to where she had left her backpack of supplies when she'd heard the scream, slowing down and keeping her ears out for any kind of warning. "From's good when it keeps you safe," she agreed. "I think we're okay here, at least for a little while. I can't hear them, at any rate. I'm Allie. Have you eaten any time recently?"

The kid shook their head, breathing hard from the run. "I'm Sam. This is Evie. She doesn't talk out loud, so don't take it personally. You have food? Real food, not just weird protein shakes? That's mostly what they gave us before. Strawberry-banana was the worst, but chocolate wasn't too bad, but I guess it's hard to make chocolate flavoured anything taste *too* bad. It's okay if you just have protein shakes, they're good, too, and give the calories for the day and efficiency is a good thing."

Allie let Sam talk until they were done, and gave Sam a friendly smile. "I have some real food. Mostly fruits and stuff like that. Do you like peaches? I have some peaches I picked a few days ago when I found an old orchard."

Sam nodded enthusiastically. "I like peaches. Evie plants fruit a lot while we walk so that other people can have food later, once it grows. Do you do that? Or is it just Evie?"

"I do it, too," Allie smiled at Sam. "It doesn't cost me much to do it, so why not? Especially if it helps other people."

Evie nodded, seeming to agree with Allie, and Allie smiled at her as well.

Allie travelled alone by choice. She liked people, but people made things messy. She didn't avoid them, she just didn't seek them out, either. She might fall in with a group for a little while, but she inevitably went her own way before too long. Part of that, a large part of it, was that Allie liked people but she did *not* trust them. But a kid changed things and while Sam wasn't the first kid that Allie had run into, it was the first time that the kid wasn't with a proper group.

"I'm sticking with you," Allie told them, though it wasn't *quite* the statement of fact that it sounded like. If they didn't want her, she'd listen but without a darn good reason, she was going with them. "You'll be safer with another person around, especially if something happens like your foot getting stuck again."

Evie signed something to Sam, and Sam translated. "Evie says you can stay with us if you want. We're not really going anywhere, though, we've mostly just been moving to keep moving."

"Me, too," Allie said, smiling at them and trying to look reassuring and not threatening. "We could go to the orchard I found, turn it into a home base? There's a lot of peaches, at least, and I bet we could build a good fence. Maybe just start small and expand out as we make sure it's safe?"

This meant her routine was going to change, but that wasn't necessarily a bad thing. It just was what it was.

The three of them took over the orchard a little bit at a time. They found the abandoned home and cleaned it up and made it livable. Allie still equated being able to get up high with being safe, since roamers couldn't climb, so they scattered blinds in various trees to make them more comfortable in an emergency. They added more gardens, vegetables and berries and gourds.

Evie was better with plants than Allie was, and she enjoyed spending time with her plant friends, and she grew more brown in the sun and smiled more often. Sam found some chickens, and Sam and Allie managed to get the chickens back to the orchard and they built a little chicken area. Sam was proud of the eggs that the hens laid and would go searching in the grass for more. Allie helped a crow with a broken wing, and the crows stayed close and brought them crow treasures. The crows even followed them on excursions and would sound a warning when roamers were nearby.

Evie still didn't talk aloud, but she laughed sometimes. Allie learned sign language so that she could understand Evie and wasn't reliant on Sam to translate. They leaned on each other and watched Sam run around chasing fireflies and learn how to be a kid even after the end of the world.

None of them talked about Life Before, but they slowly put down roots where they were. The orchard turned into The Orchard, where it became home and they became a family. They'd leave for short trips sometimes, to plant new gardens for other people because even if they wouldn't see the results they wanted to help something bigger than themselves.

Sometimes they found people and brought them back, and other times people showed up, but either way, people needed a safe space to rest before they moved on. Allie and Evie built a little house for new people to stay in, so that they didn't have to let strangers stay in their home but could still give them safety.

No one stayed long, though sometimes people would come back for a few days every once in a while.

They helped whenever they could, because it was the right thing to do, but they didn't trust.

Sam always stayed close to Evie and Allie when the three of them went out on excursions, but Sam's definition of close and their definition of close wasn't always the same thing. They probably gave Sam a little too much leeway, but Sam could run and Sam could climb, so Sam wasn't really in a lot of danger from the roamers. The biggest danger was people, but even with society in tatters, most people did not want to hurt children.

They usually stayed at The Orchard, because most of the time there wasn't a pressing need to leave. Even so, every few weeks, they'd gather new plants, pick up any people they found that needed help, and plant some seeds for fruits and vegetables and berries for future people to stumble onto. Allie or Sam made sure to stay with Evie, just so that in case something happened, Evie was with someone who could get loud. Evie still wasn't talking aloud, but she was vocalizing more and that was a good thing, right? It wasn't like Sam had much knowledge to draw from for selective mutism, other than to know that the term was somewhat misleading, but it seemed like a good thing to Sam, so Sam was going to mark it off as progress.

Sam jumped over a fallen tree and let out a cry of surprise when the ground was lower than expected, sprawling out on the dirt because their ankle crumpled underneath them.

It only seemed to be a few seconds before Allie was right next to Sam, looking at Sam's ankle with gentle fingers and probing carefully. "Seems to be a strain, not a full sprain. It won't feel good, but you can walk on it, long as you're careful." Allie smoothed some hair out of Sam's face with a small smile. "Let me wrap it up and then we'll start heading back home."

Sam nodded and tried to hold still while Allie did the wrapping, but Sam had *never* been good at sitting still, so it was pretty much a lost cause doomed to fail before it even started.

Evie touched Allie's shoulder, frowning as she looked for whatever was worrying her. Sure, they could hear some roamers in the distance, but they already knew about that.

It wasn't actually easy to be ambushed by a roamer if you could hear. They made a *lot* of noise, which attracted other zombies to them, and they formed packs like that. So it was easy to hear the roamers and easy to avoid them as a result. The problem came in when there were two groups converging, since it was harder to know which direction was safe.

They could hear at least three groups.

And Sam couldn't run, thanks to the newly busted ankle.

Okay. Running was not a great option, but they could still get up high. High meant safe, since the zombies couldn't climb. If the roamers even noticed the three of them, they'd stay around the tree until they got distracted, but that was about all they could do, and they were pretty easy to distract. "Climb?" Sam suggested, standing to test whether or not their ankle would hold up.

Evie nodded at Sam, scanning for movement, while Allie packed the supplies back up into her bag. "Climb," Allie agreed, shifting the backpack around on her back to get it to settle comfortably.

Evie was the tallest, so she threw a climbing rope over a sturdy branch, looping it easily like they'd all practiced over and over at Allie's insistence.

Sam knew the rules and the order, so Sam scrambled up the rope quickly, before continuing on to another branch higher up so that Evie could start following. Evie had argued with Allie multiple times before about the order, but for all of Allie's cheerfulness, she was surprisingly stubborn when she felt like she had to be. When it came to Sam and Evie's safety, Allie felt like she had to be, so she dug her heels in and refused to move them.

Allie climbed to the first branch without any problems, the three of them safely in the tree and clustered around the trunk from different sides to balance it out as much as possible. Allie unlooped the rope and coiled it up and clipped it to her belt until she could give it back to Evie. The problem came after that, when Allie tried to climb to a new branch to the other side of the tree from Evie. She tested it first, the same way they always did, but tests weren't a guarantee. While Allie was shifting to get comfortable, the branch underneath her cracked and plummeted to the ground without warning, taking Allie with it.

Allie let out a sharp scream as she fell, the sound morphing to a cry of pain when she hit the ground.

"Allie!" Sam started to get ready to jump down to check on her.

"Don't you *even dare*," Allie snapped at Sam without looking up. "You stay right where you are, Samford Sammerson."

That was not even a little bit Sam's name. Sam was just a Sam, but Sam reluctantly settled back down because joke name or not, it *did* mean that Allie was serious and it was a Full Name-ing kind of situation.

"Toss the rope and we'll pull you up," Sam suggested, panic edging into their voice.

"I don't think that's exactly an option," Allie admitted, rolling over so they could see the issue. Namely that her arm was bent backwards and a bone was protruding where a bone should definitely not be poking.

Evie let out a noise of dismay, and Sam scrabbled through their own backpack to find something, *anything*, to help get Allie up into the tree. "Well, we're not leaving you, so figure something out."

"It'll be okay," Allie said softly as she climbed to her feet, her face white with pain and her eyes glassy.

"This is so not okay!" Sam yelled over the noise from the roamers getting closer. "This is the opposite of okay, so figure something out and *move your butt*."

Allie shook her head, gripping her arm until her knuckles turned white. "It's okay. I can lead them away from you guys. You'll be safe, and that's the important part."

"No." Sam stated it flatly. "No, you don't get to do this." Sam turned to Evie, falling back on the way they'd first communicated with each other, before Sam had learned sign language. ::*we have to risk it. Allie won't… she's not like that. we can't let her do this, so we have to trust her.*::

Evie nodded. ::*but you have to stay up here. i can't focus and be worried about you.*:: She dropped down out of the tree, landing soundlessly next to Allie.

"No!" Allie looked like she was about two seconds away from bursting into tears. "Climb back up! You can't… you *can't*. Get back into that tree!"

Evie shook her head and kissed Allie hard but fast, since they didn't have much time to prepare.

"Evie says you're being stupid, she loves you, she's not leaving you, but it *will* be okay," Sam told Allie.

Allie gave Sam a confused look, clearly shocky from her arm. "But she didn't sign anything."

"Nope," Sam agreed. "She says to stay still and quiet, keep holding on to her, try to stay calm, and trust her. I'm under strict orders to stay up here."

Allie nodded at Evie, leaning their foreheads together. "Always. Always trust you," she promised.

They'd never tried with a big group before. There was no guarantee. ::*what if this doesn't work?*:: Sam asked Evie, needing some reassurance.

Evie and Allie never lied to Sam, even if Sam sometimes wished they would. But it meant that when one of them said things would be okay, Sam could trust it. ::*it will. it will because it has to work. i have to be able to do this, so therefore i am able, because i can* not *fail at this. It's not an option. Now hush and let me concentrate.*::

Sam bit their lip in worry but tried to not think too loudly, humming for Evie instead to give her a focus.

Evie hummed with Sam, and Sam could feel Evie *push out* with the hum. It was a lot, it was so much more than anything they'd tried before, but it was working. The roamers were moving past them without paying any attention to Evie, even though some of them were so close they were actually brushing against the two of them as they passed by.

But Sam could tell that it wouldn't be enough, and Sam couldn't sit and do nothing. So even though Evie would *kill* Sam for it, they tied themself to the tree and hummed louder at Evie, pushing energy to Evie.

Evie resisted, but Sam refused to take it back. Evie started to flag like Sam knew she would,and Sam pushed harder. Evie reluctantly accepted it, shaping it and retwisting it and spreading it out to the roamers to keep them moving.

Sam kept pushing towards Evie, and Evie kept pushing towards the roamers, and finally the last zombie disappeared into the trees.

They held perfectly still a little longer, ears peeled for warning that the roamers were changing directions and coming back.

Satisfied that they were safe, Evie glared up at Sam, gesturing sharply at Sam. *Get down,* she signed. *Right now. You are grounded for the rest of your natural life.*

"I don't even go anywhere anyway," Sam pointed out, untying the rope and climbing down with a sigh. "Besides, you needed it and you know it."

"Not the point," Evie's hands moved sharp and fast, showing just how *mad* she was, because Evie's signing was usually fluid. *"I told you I needed to concentrate and I couldn't if I was worried about you."*

"I tied myself so you wouldn't worry about me falling. I'm not sorry so I'm not going to apologize," Sam said mulishly. "Now lemme help Allie."

Allie blinked at the two of them, understanding what was being said but she still didn't have the context to make the words make sense. "What the *hell*?"

"Surprise?" Sam shrugged. "We have nifty tricks. But it's hard. This was kind of an emergency situation. Now lemme look at your arm."

Allie obediently held her arm out, biting her lip to stay quiet.

Sam hummed, the same note from before, letting things build. They probably didn't actually *need* the humming, but the humming had been part of the process for so long, and Sam had learned by using the hum to focus. At this point, the humming was a focal tool that Sam didn't know how to *not* use. Satisfied that everything had reached the point that it needed to, Sam started adjusting Allie's arm, pulling things back into place and knitting them back together.

Sam wasn't sure how long it took, they tended to zone out when healing, but when they opened their eyes they were all sweaty and gross so it had probably been a while. "It's going to hurt for a while," Sam warned Allie. "It's still healing. This just gets you about a two week head start. I can do better usually, but it was a bad break and if I push too much more, Evie'll kill me."

"I think Evie's already planning on killing you," Allie pointed out, her eyes already clearer from the pain. "Even if I don't know what you did, I'm pretty sure I'm planning on killing you, too. Evie has good judgment on that."

Sam glowered at them both. "Can we just go home? Evie and I'll explain on the way. But I'm hungry now and I want to sleep for a week."

"Cliff notes version?" Allie suggested, tucking herself under Sam's arm to help bear Sam's weight since Sam's ankle still hurt.

"And why couldn't you do that for yourself?"

Sam shrugged. "Doesn't work on myself. Besides, the ankle's not too bad. I just don't think I can run on it. Cliff notes is that Evie can ...redirect them, I guess. She can keep them from noticing her, or make them notice something else instead."

"And what did you do to piss her off?" Allie arched an eyebrow at Sam and waited Sam out.

"It was a big group. Evie's never tried with more than a few. She didn't have enough… whatever it is we use. We say energy but who knows what it really is. So I gave her some and I'm *not sorry about it*," Sam glared at Evie on the last bit.

"Grounded," Evie signed, "*rest of your natural life. So grounded.*"

"Still needed me," Sam grumbled, but the three of them started walking back to The Orchard.

Allie would like to think that she took everything in stride, once they reassured her that they hadn't kept it from her because they didn't trust her, but because they didn't know how to start telling her. She had questions, of course, and they tried to answer them.

Allie and Evie don't talk about the kiss, or Sam telling Allie that Evie said she loved Allie. But it didn't need *talking about, not really. It wasn't like they ignored it, they just filed it away and kept moving forwards.*

They talked about other stuff. They talked about how Evie couldn't remember much before the experiments, or even much about them. They talked about how guilty Evie felt, not fighting back or trying to escape until they brought Sam in and told Evie to work with Sam. They talked about how Evie had been so angry *that they would experiment on a* child *that she had created an opportunity and grabbed Sam and ran, refusing to look back. They talked about how shortly after Allie and Sam escaped, the zombie outbreak started, and Evie always wondered after that if it was her fault, if the first roamer got out because of something Evie did.*

Allie helped reassure Evie a lot *after that.*

They talked about Allie, even though she felt like her stuff was a lot smaller than government experiments. But they talked about Allie, growing up youngest in a big family and how she sometimes felt like an afterthought to her parents. They talked about how her oldest brother, Jordan, was more of a parent than their actual parents; Jordan was the one that made cupcakes for her bake sales or class birthdays, and Jordan was the one that ran her birthday parties, or braided her hair for her. They talked about how scary it had been for Allie to have a bad case of the flu and when she'd surfaced again, the world had ended. They talked about how Jordan had done so much for Allie and now Allie didn't even know where Jordan was or even if he was still alive.

They talked about a lot of things, important and unimportant, even though, really, it was all *important, but they didn't talk about love.*

They didn't need to.

The three of them conducted their own experiments, a little at a time. They built a big pen to hold some roamers and Evie redirected some small groups into it without any problems. Bigger groups were harder, until Evie learned that if she focused on the first ones in the group, the others would follow those ones.

The big change came when Sam tried to heal a roamer to see what would happen, since the worst case scenario was "nothing". It wasn't a lot, *in Sam's opinion. They were still zombies. But they were calmer, they didn't try to attack people, and they could even do rote, repetitive tasks.*

They named the roamers and let them do small jobs that needed doing but it was okay if they weren't done perfectly, like tilling for planting.

This gave Evie hope that a cure might even be found for the zombies, so they tried harder to round roamers up instead of letting them continue on where they might hurt people. They had to build more pens, and Sam was only allowed to heal once, maybe twice, a day, so it wasn't a fast change, but things did change.

Word spread about their little group, the zombie whisperer and the healer, and it was met with a lot of disbelief, but sometimes to get anything started, you just need to give people something to believe in and hope for.

Everything changed even more with Susan.

Evie had a routine. She had a reason for it; she did better when she had a routine to stick to and it helped her not get so anxious or feel out of control of things. She didn't have to worry about whether or not she'd done something that needed doing if she did it at more or less the same time. Every few weeks, they'd leave to go check on the places they'd planted various foods, see what took root and what needed a little more help before it was fully self-sufficient. They would also rescue any animals or people that needed the help, but by setting the other goals, every trip could always be termed a success. The regular trips also helped them keep track of when things happened, because when every day was the same, time had a tendency to smush and blend together.

It was an excursion day. Where Sam used to run ahead but stay in sight, Sam now seemed to stick in close to them, scouting ahead if asked but preferring to stay with them. Part of Evie was sad that Sam worried now when they hadn't before, but Evie was also relieved that Sam would be in less danger as a result. But Evie and Allie had worked hard to give Sam a sense of safety, and Evie felt like she'd failed at that now, but Sam hadn't changed their behavior at The Orchard. They were still a *kid*, maybe not a typical one but Sam wasn't exactly typical to begin with. Sam still ran around The Orchard, taking care of the chickens and catching fireflies to let go again. Sam didn't really trust their guests, but Sam was polite and despite that lack of trust, Sam didn't *worry*, because Sam knew that The Orchard was safe. So maybe Evie wasn't failing Sam after all.

Evie's job was listening out, so when she heard a noise that was definitely not a roamer, she signalled Allie and Sam to stay wary but gestured in the direction of the moan.

"Hello?" Allie called out, taking point with a new person the way she always did. Evie found them but Allie was the one who'd talk to them. *Occasionally* Sam, but that was pretty rare.

Sam really didn't trust new people. Allie had been the exception to that rule.

"Yes? Hello?" Whoever answered was clearly in distress, which made Evie frown.

"We're coming to help," Allie announced, following the voice until they reached the other woman.

She was dirty and sweaty, and she was also *very very pregnant*, and Evie was pretty sure she was actively in labour.

Evie looked to Allie. *"The Orchard will be safest, but only if we can get her there. We're not too far away, but it just depends on if she can walk or not."*

Allie nodded at Evie, and focused back on the other woman. "I'm Allie, this is Evie and Sam, and we're going to help you. Evie doesn't talk out loud, so don't take it personally. If you can walk, we'd like to get you back to our place, it has more supplies and it's not very far from here. If you can't, we'll just make do with what we have."

"Susan," the lady introduced herself, gritting her teeth through another contraction. "I can walk, but it won't be fast."

"That's not a problem," Allie gave Susan a reassuring smile. "We'll help you." She tucked herself on one side of Susan, and Evie did the same on the other, so that the two of them could bear as much of Susan's weight as possible.

Susan hadn't been lying, it *was* slow going, but Allie hadn't been lying when she said it wasn't a problem, either. They had to stop when a bad contraction hit, which seemed to be often. Sam would scout ahead at those points, though they stayed within Evie's and Allie's line of sight and moved carefully to make sure they didn't risk accidental injury.

"You're doing great," Allie encouraged Susan with a bright smile. "We're almost there, and then you won't have to worry about roamers or anything like that, and you can just focus on having that baby of yours."

Evie nodded in agreement, holding out some water for Susan if she wanted it. Susan accepted it with a grateful nod in return, taking a few swallows before passing it back, and Evie clipped it to her belt again, before catching Allie's eye. *"I think we're close enough that we can send Sam ahead to get people to help carry Susan,"* she signed.

"We'll hear if Sam calls for help," Allie agreed with a sigh, clearly not liking the solution but recognizing the benefits to it. "Sam!"

Sam ran back at Allie's call, giving them an expectant look.

"We need you to run back to The Orchard," Evie explained, her hands moving fluidly from sign to sign. *"Get at least two of the strong and fast guys to come back with the stretcher. We're close enough that we can hear you if you call."*

Sam nodded at Evie, their eyes wide but their jaw resolute. "You stay safe, too, okay? I don't want anything happening to *you*, either."

"Promise," Evie signed to Sam, holding her pinky up for a pinky-promise, shaking their hands together when Sam linked their pinky with Evie's.

Sam tugged Evie in for a quick hug, following it with a hug to Allie, before disengaging with another sigh, and loped off.

Allie and Evie helped Susan walk some more, while Evie kept an ear out for Sam or the roamers. For all that Evie had only had Sam for a few years, Sam was still her child in the ways that mattered, and Evie worried about Sam, even if logically she knew that Sam was just about as safe as it was possible to guarantee. Evie wouldn't have suggested that Sam do something dangerous, after all, and Allie wouldn't have agreed to it.

But Evie still worried. That was part of being a parent.

They were stopped again for Susan to breathe through another contraction when Sam came running back, Jacob and Tyler following with the stretcher. Evie wasn't usually very touchy-feely with Sam, preferring to let Sam initiate hugs and such, but she was relieved to have Sam back in sight, and opened her arms for a hug if Sam wanted it. While Jake and Ty got Susan situated, Sam leaned into the hug and squeezed Evie tight, so Sam was probably in the same boat as Evie.

"This is Jacob and Tyler,"Allie introduced them to Susan, "they can carry you no problem, so don't worry, and it'll be a lot faster. It'll be a lot easier on you now, too, so all you need to do is focus on yourself and that baby of yours."

Susan nodded at Allie, breathing heavily, and Evie recognized the rhythm and started breathing with Susan, hoping that it helped. Jake and Ty picked the stretcher up easily and started off to The Orchard, and Sam decided to start timing Susan's contractions. By the time they arrived, it was clear that Susan was in full-blown labour, though that hadn't actually been in doubt.

"We don't have any doctors or anything like that," Allie told Susan, a note of apology in her voice, "but we'll do what we can, and I'll ask if anyone has any type of experience with birth."

"Lila's a vet, and Julie's sister had a home birth and Julie was her birthing partner," Sam volunteered. "I asked already, and they both said that they'll do what they can to help."

"Better than being in the woods by myself," Susan pointed out.

"That's true! It's a *lot* better than being in the woods. We have clean water we can boil, and plenty of soap, so it'll definitely be cleaner," Allie agreed cheerfully.

Julie and Lila already had boiled water cooling off and more water boiling when they got Susan into the house. Once Susan got settled, Allie caught Evie's eye and gestured outside, so Evie followed Allie.

"I think you and Sam should stay out here," Allie told Evie in a quiet voice, worrying her lower lip between her teeth. "If anything goes wrong, I don't want Sam in there, and you'd be best at making sure Sam *actually* stays out. You know how Sam gets when they're convinced they need to help."

Evie gave Allie a wary look. *"What are you trying to get around telling me?"*

Allie sighed, reaching out to touch Evie's cheek lightly. "I'm not sure how to say this without it coming out *wrong*, so please just… keep that in mind, and that however bad it sounds, that's not how I mean it?" Evie nodded, and Allie gave her a soft smile. "Thanks, baby. There's going to be a lot of ferrying things, including the boiling water, and that's going to mean a lot of communication with each other so that we know where we all are and don't collide or knock into anyone."

Despite the warning, Evie couldn't keep the hurt off her face. *"You think I'll be in the way?"* she signed, her hands almost drooping.

"Baby, *no*," Allie said firmly. "This is what I was trying to avoid. I don't think you're a problem. If it was just the three of us helping, I think you'd be the best one to have in there. But for people who aren't used to you and aren't going to be paying attention, it's just not a good idea. And I think we both agree that the priority here is Susan and her baby."

Evie *did* agree there, so she nodded at Allie. Her feelings were still a little hurt, though she thought it was mostly by the situation and her own feelings about her limitations and not actually because of what

Allie had said. Not for the first time, she wished she knew *why* she couldn't talk and why the words froze in her throat. (Trauma. The answer was trauma. Evie just didn't like the answer.) She tried, but… this was the way it was, and maybe it would change and maybe it wouldn't, but wishing wouldn't be the thing that changed it.

"Hey," Allie kissed her soft and gentle, leaning her forehead on Evie's. "Nothing wrong with you. I know that face, that's your '*I don't think I'm good enough or cause problems*' face, and neither of those things are true, okay? I love you, and that means I love you as you are. I don't *care* that you don't speak verbally, other than how it makes you feel. I mean it. I wouldn't change *anything* about you." Allie paused for a moment. "Except your feet. They get too cold and you put them up against me because you hate sleeping in socks. I would absolutely change that. But that's it, just the socks thing."

Evie couldn't help but laugh at that, the sound wispy like fog on a sunny morning, and she kissed Allie's nose and pulled away with a sigh. *"Go help with Susan. I'll stay with Sam, and you come get us if we're needed."*

Allie nodded and kissed Evie again before she pulled away and headed into the house.

Maybe Evie might have to stay *outside*, but she could at least keep water topped up so that someone who could be helping Susan wouldn't have to be fetching it, so she set about doing that. Sam stayed in close against Evie while they waited for any news.

Evie wasn't sure how many buckets they'd ferried from the well to the house, or how much time had passed before Allie came out to get them. "Susan and the baby seem to be doing okay and we got them cleaned up. Susan wanted you two to be the next to meet Baby Hope."

Evie and Sam followed Allie, both of them staying quiet.

Susan held her new baby in close, and she looked up at them and smiled. "This is Hope. Hope, these people helped you get here."

"She looks like a baby should look," Sam nodded, as though Sam had any idea about babies, but Evie wasn't going to be the one to point it out.

Evie nodded in agreement, signing a very simple *"Beautiful,"* for Allie to translate.

Susan kept petting Hope's hair, but her smile melted away, replaced by worry. "How long can I stay? If everybody else is temporary…"

"As long as you want," Allie promised. "We'll make it work. You have a *baby*. We're not going to kick you out or make you fend for yourself."

Allie had told Evie that Sam was the one that changed things for Allie. Before Sam, Allie wanted to stay on the move even if she didn't know what she was looking for, but after Sam, Allie just wanted to make sure Sam was safe.

Evie thought that Hope was causing the same reaction that Sam had. They had set up the houses for temporary guests because they didn't want to deal with people and the headaches that came with them long term. There were always fights for power, and Evie and Allie didn't want to *deal* with that. But just like Sam had, Hope needed safety, and Evie already knew they'd do everything they could to make that happen.

"We'll need to build a new house for Susan and Hope," Evie signed to Allie, *"and we don't have any baby things so we'll need to repurpose things or make new things."*

Allie nodded at Evie. "We'll make it work," she repeated, her voice strong with conviction.

It looked like Evie's routine was going to change, too. And that wasn't a bad thing.

They'd make it work.

More people start staying after Susan and Hope do. It starts slow, but just like everything else Evie and Allie and Sam have done, it gains traction and speed. Not everyone they rescue stays with them, but usually the ones that move on are the ones that are looking for a specific person or trying to reach a particular place. The ones looking for safety or stability opt to stay, more often than not.

When people move on, they invariably talk about The Orchard, and what the ladies and that kid are up to, what they've accomplished, humans and zombies together, can you believe it? The idea takes hold, and other communities start recreating the parts that they can. There aren't many zombie whisperers, since they were the result of experiments, and even less healers, but the whisperers find homes quickly enough and move the roamers to their own areas so that they'll be ready when a cure is found.

Evie made it happen, through faith, hope, and sheer determination, because she refused to allow it to not work.

A network forms, with runners moving from community to community to share information or memorize messages to pass on. They don't carry things, *because that would weigh them down. Even letters would turn into luggage that the runners would have to carry. Runners have to stay light to stay fast, so they don't carry anything they don't absolutely have to. Among the things they have to, though, is a list of people and who is looking for who. It's how Allie finds out that Jordan is okay and she invites him to come join them at The Orchard. He's entirely unsurprised to find out that Allie is one of the "lesbian plant moms" he's heard about. He shows up with his new family and wants to get to know Evie and Sam.*

One of their visitors throws a rock at one of the roamers one day and Evie has to intercept when Sam starts to round on the guest. While Evie's holding on to Sam, Allie unceremoniously kicks him out, and says that anyone who thinks it's okay to throw a rock at someone that hasn't done anything to them can get out, too. Unsurprisingly no one accepts that offer.

Their roamers are under their protection and they don't take that responsibility lightly.

One man challenges Allie on whether or not Allie and Evie should be in charge of The Orchard. Allie's response is to knock him on his ass without warning, and when he looks up at her, Allie's sword is in her hand and the tip is against his throat to show what she could *do if she had to. She pulls it back quickly because while she will if she has to, she* doesn't *have to. He drops it and no one challenges them again. Allie and Evie are in charge and what they say goes, though they promise to be as fair as they can be.*

More communities take on the same rules that Evie and Allie set up, which mostly revolve around helping when you can and respecting other people and yes "captured" zombies count as people for this. More people want that than want a wasteland that they can rule, so more and more, people do what they can to help others and trust that others will help them.

The world begins to change again.

Maybe it's not a big difference. Maybe it's just throwing starfish back into the sea even when you can't save them all. Maybe it doesn't make a measurable difference to the world as a whole. But it makes ***all*** *the difference to each rescued starfish, and in some way, aren't we all stranded starfishes hoping for help?*

Maybe it's not a difference. But maybe it's all *the difference.*

CHASING RABBITS – KAT DODD

Chase Arledge sat in the dark, sorting through the deluge of information from the Net that her programs and codes had gathered for her while she was at school. It was easier to process what she was seeing over her ocular implant if there were fewer visual distractions. She probably could have had her light on, but she was still getting used to her implant, so the dark suited her purposes just fine. She was determined to find an answer this time, even though every night went more or less the same, and she'd never found *anything*.

But tonight would be different. It *had* to be. Not because of a time crunch, but because Chase had been trying for seven years (and trying harder for four), and at some point, even *her* relentless determination and optimism would fail. She'd gotten better at it over the years, of course, but...

It still felt like failure, and Chase wasn't a failure.

She *refused* to be.

Chase jumped when her door opened, and she blinked rapidly at her mom, hoping that Mary Elizabeth hadn't seen the tell-tale glare of the implant. Sitting in the dark wasn't exactly a normal thing for Chase to do, and her brain was scrambling to think of an excuse that wouldn't be *stupid*. "I had a migraine," she blurted out.

Apparently, that was the exact wrong thing to say, because even though Mary Elizabeth believed her, she spent the next three hours checking in on Chase and making her drink water to fix the migraine, even though that *never* worked, and Chase was tense and on edge because she never knew when her mom would come in, and she was somewhat terrified that her mom would see the slight glow of the implant and realize what Chase had done. For all that she was eighteen and technically able to make her own decisions now, she still wasn't allowed more tech than what she absolutely *needed* for school. Even that was still just barely and begrudgingly acceptable, and Chase just really didn't want that fight to kick off yet again, especially since she didn't even have anything to show for her actions yet.

Yet. She was determined for it to be a 'yet'.

Besides, her parents weren't really interested in her life, anyway. So long as she didn't reflect badly on them, so long as she did what she was supposed to do and didn't make waves, they didn't care about *her*. Sure, they cared about if she was hurting, at least physically, but Chase didn't think they knew anything about what she liked or didn't like. Like dinner that night had been beef, and Chase was a vegetarian. So either they didn't care enough to know that she no longer ate meat, or they knew but didn't care enough to adjust.

Either way? It came down to "they didn't care".

Maybe it was unkind, but being unkind didn't keep it from being the truth, and checking in on her to see if she was doing better was more to make Mary Elizabeth feel better about being a good mom than actually helping Chase . Otherwise Mary Elizabeth would leave Chase be, let her stay in the dark and try to ride out the migraine. Which Mary Elizabeth should know since Chase was no stranger to migraines and they *knew* what worked and what didn't work. Meds, lie down in a cool, quiet, dark place, and try to "sleep" it off even if she didn't sleep. But can't have meds in the Arledge house, no, everything must be all natural. Can't leave Chase alone, no, must check on her and make sure she's okay.

Like she said. More to assuage Mary Elizabeth 's own feelings than actually help Chase .

Finally, *finally*, Mary Elizabeth and Matthew went to bed, the noises from the living room going quiet as they moved to their own room.

Chase relaxed slowly. The worry that she'd be caught using her implant any moment had caused a tension headache, so the first thing Chase did was try to stretch it out and the second thing she did was take some over the counter headache medication.

Hey, her parents believed in all natural. *She* did not. So far as Chase was concerned, it was a tool to be used when you needed it and she needed it.

She fell into a rote routine of looking at the picture or text her codes had found and moving on when it was obvious that it didn't apply to her search, and her mind started to wander. She needed to pay closer attention, but it was hard when she never found *anything*. Maybe she needed to narrow her search parameters further, but then she was afraid that she'd miss something important.

She almost flicked past the picture automatically, before it registered what she was looking at.

This wasn't from seven years ago, like she'd been looking for. This was from seven *hours* ago.

She hadn't found out how or why Leverett disappeared. She'd found proof that he was still alive.

To say she was surprised would be an understatement.

What. The. Frell?

If he was still alive then why hadn't he tried to talk to her? Why had he just left?

Okay. First steps first. Make absolutely sure that this is Leverett, that it's not just a picture of someone that looks like Leverett. After all, a lot of people have doppelgangers. Maybe she'd found Leverett's. No use to jump to conclusions before she verified anything, right?

But no, the deeper she dug, the more she'd found until Chase had printed off a thick packet of proof that it was actually Leverett and information on his life since he'd disappeared. Some things didn't match up with what she'd been told, but, hey, she'd just found out that the older brother she'd near worshipped and idolized wasn't actually dead after all, and that was a doozy of a discrepancy.

Chase set everything in order to talk to her parents about it in the morning, and tried to go to sleep. She wasn't sure how long she lay there in the dark, her thoughts spiralling, but eventually she managed to drift off.

Morning came a lot sooner than Chase wanted and she grumbled at the Looney Toons alarm clock she'd had for as long as she could remember. It was earlier than she *needed* to be up, but she wanted to be the first one out so she could talk to her parents. She didn't want to have to wait a whole day to talk about what she'd found, and she *really* didn't want to go to school when she still had so many questions. Chase set the printed information on the kitchen table before getting her breakfast ready.

Mary Elizabeth was the next to come out, her white suit immaculate and not a blonde hair out of place. "What's this, dear? Something from school?" She glanced at it, though she was distracted by fastening her bracelet.

"No, not for school," Chase said. She didn't have to go on, though, because she could see the exact moment that her mother realized what it was.

"Matthew! Come talk to your daughter! *Now*." Mary Elizabeth deliberately turned her back on Chase, making herself some coffee.

But if it hadn't been coffee, it would have been something else, because the real point was that Chase's mother didn't want to look at her.

"What's all the shouting about?" Matthew came out, more than a little befuddled by the situation.

"Ask Chase what bombshell she decided to drop this morning," Mary Elizabeth said coldly, her eyes steely when she turned back around.

Chase didn't know what kind of reaction she'd expected, but it wasn't *this*. She knew they'd be mad at her for not dropping it when they'd told her over and over to and to stop digging up old ghosts, but this was a level of anger that she hadn't anticipated. Chase squared her shoulders, prepared to face it head on, though. She'd pushed this far, she wasn't about to turn tail and run. "I know you don't like it when I bring up Leverett, but I found out he's alive."

Almost exactly as Mary Elizabeth had, Matthew went still and cold, gray eyes turning to flint and his mouth getting a hard set to it. "Why can't you ever *listen*?" he demanded. "We told you to *drop it* for a reason."

That was like getting smacked to the face with a wet towel. "You knew?" Chase felt like her world was splintering around her, and everything she'd believed was put into question.

"It doesn't matter," Mary Elizabeth insisted firmly, her hands steady again. "It happened so long ago, and he never tried to come back or talk to you, did he? He made his choice, and we miss him, of course, but he's the one who…" she trailed off. "It was his choice," she repeated, less convinced this time but just as firm.

"We've talked about this enough. It's time we all leave. You are not allowed to keep looking into this, and we *will* discuss punishment tonight." Matthew turned away, already dismissing Chase.

Mary Elizabeth nodded, scooping up all the information Chase had prepared and unceremoniously dropping it in the trash can.

Chase didn't move while her parents left. If they thought she was going to leave it be after all this, they knew her about as well as she thought they did.

Once she was certain they'd left for work, Chase pulled the papers out of the trash before she started packing up her things. She was going to Leverett, she had an address and a lot of questions, and damn it, she was going to get some answers.

Despite not getting much sleep the night before, Chase was wide awake when she left the town limits. For some reason, she'd expected it to be harder to leave, but, no, all she had to do was drive and not stop.

Maybe that was hard enough.

All her life, Chase's parents had told her that the world was too dependent on technology, and that their town was the only safe area left. If they'd had their way, she would have been homeschooled and not been introduced to any computers, like how they'd grown up, but times had changed and homeschooling was no longer an option (probably because of people like New Haven's residents, who wouldn't have taught necessary things). She'd always been told that the things she'd see on the Net was a lie, that it was all propaganda and she shouldn't trust it.

And she *hadn't* trusted it. She couldn't see it in person, and that meant she didn't know whether or not it actually existed. She liked to put her trust in things she could see with her own eyes or touch herself, not in things that could be faked.

But now she was looking at *actual flying cars*, and it was overwhelming enough that she had to pull over. It wasn't *just* flying cars, of course, there were plenty of ground vehicles like her own, so she didn't stick out like a sore thumb. But it was enough for her to know that it was *true* and not just lies to make people want to leave New Haven like she'd been told.

And it made her wonder what else she'd believed that were only lies in the end. If her parents could tell her that Leverett was dead when he wasn't, if they could tell her that the technology didn't really exist when it did, what else had they told her that was a lie?

Was it more lies than truth?

It took a few days for Chase to get from Arizona to New York. She *could* have gone faster, if she'd decided to, but she was seeing all of this for the first time and she was taking it all in, and besides, she was a big fan of sleep. Even if she was mostly sleeping in her car because she didn't want to spend too much on motels; she had more than enough money to *get* her to Leverett, but she didn't want to drain her funds, either.

It was also possible that she was procrastinating more than a little bit because she didn't know what to say to Leverett once she got there. *"Hi, I'm the sister you abandoned and never tried to contact, what the hell?"* was probably not the best place to start, but she couldn't get past it, either, so that's what her brain was stuck on. She *tried* to think of other things, but that's what she kept cycling back to.

It all turned out to be a moot point anyway, since when she got there nobody answered the door. Leverett was probably at work, and *no*, she was *not* about to just drop in on him at work when she had no idea if he even wanted to see her. She'd found where he worked, but *no*. Not happening.

Chase thought about going back to her car and waiting there, but she worried she'd miss him if she did that, so she just sat on his doorstep and waited and tried to think of something else to say when he got there.

Or at least, that was the plan, because what really wound up happening was that she fell asleep.

Well, "sleep" was an exaggeration, because even Chase knew not to fall asleep in a strange place when she was outside. That just seemed like a good way to get robbed. Or a good way to get *dead.* She liked not being dead. She *dozed*, which probably wasn't that much safer but made her feel better than falling asleep would.

Not like it was planned.

Whatever you wanted to call it, Chase woke up when she heard someone saying her name.

She didn't have time to say any of the things she'd tried to think of before Leverett was hugging her tightly -- because it had to be Leverett even if she hadn't had a chance to see his face yet -- and she could feel her shirt getting damp from his tears. "I was hoping you'd find me," he told her as he squeezed her tight.

"Then why did you leave?" It wasn't where she'd meant to start, but… well, that was the crux of it, so she wasn't going to backpedal and try to rephrase. "Why didn't you ever try to talk to me? They said you were *dead.*"

"Chase." Leverett pulled away, sounding stricken, face pale. "I left for college. That's all. I wasn't allowed back because you know how Mom and Dad are about things. They don't believe in technology but you're like me. You know that there's more than we were taught."

"How do you know?" Chase could hear the challenge in her voice.

Leverett gave her a soft smile. "You found me. I've been trying to leave a trail for you to find, if you wanted to, and you did or you wouldn't be here. That's *proof* that you haven't bought into their bull hockey. There's more to the world than they wanted us to believe, and you know it because you're here. The only question now is if you want to see the world as it *really* is, or if you want to go back home."

Chase hadn't thought about what she'd do once she actually found Leverett. Maybe she'd thought they would go back home together, but if he'd wanted to go back, he would have years ago. What was there for her? A life she didn't know in a world that she didn't understand? Or a future where almost everything was settled but she'd always know what she was missing, with people who'd lied to her all her life?

It sounded like it should be an easy choice on paper, but they were still her parents and she didn't know if she could just turn her back on them.

But she'd *just* found Leverett and didn't think she could turn her back on *him*, either.

The world was bigger than she'd been taught, and that was more than a little bit terrifying.

But Chase had never been one to give in to fear. Her reaction to fear was to face it head on until it didn't scare her anymore.

The world was bigger than she'd been taught, and that was more than a little bit exhilarating.

Chase squared her shoulders and lifted her chin. "I want to see the truth."

Maybe she'd be able to reach some of her friends in New Haven. After all, Leverett disappearing could be explained, mostly by no one ever talking about it ever. Chase disappearing as well was a lot harder. It would raise flags, invite questions. Maybe people would look for her and she could scatter better breadcrumbs for them than Leverett had for her.

The more people that followed, the more it would make other people question and look into it themselves. Either they'd change

New Haven themselves or they'd leave and that would still result in change.

Maybe Chase was being optimistic, but… A revolution doesn't start with everything all ready. It starts with one person saying they're done, until more people join in.

Maybe Chase had found her revolution.

FULL-FLEDGED HOPE – AXEL KELLY

The ship lurched around me at another near-miss, and I gripped the arm-rests of my seat. "How much longer until we can jump again?" I demanded.

Petra looked back at me, her face a ghostly blue from the light of the computer screen. "Another minute, maybe two," her voice was distracted.

The *Esperanza* lurched again, as another missile detonated close to our port side. It had been fired from the ship that had pursued us for days – one of the many corporate-run security craft that were usually one hundred percent successful in preventing people from leaving Sol.

"We might want to be a bit faster than that, love," I said, doing my best to keep my voice light. "If it weren't for the fact that these people couldn't hit a barn door from three yards, we'd already be pulverised dust floating in space."

"I know, but there's only so much I can do with a ship that was secretly rebuilt using replacement parts from recycling dumps."

I grimaced. My partner made a damned good point, unfortunately. I hoped the other Exodus Flight ships were doing okay, and that none was lying motionless in the cold, empty eternity of space or, indeed, adding to its micro-detritus as I feared we might shortly be doing.

"Just do your best. Our blooming autocannon haven't even

scratched that pursuit ship. I..."

Another near-impact stopped me mid-sentence. The ship had, once again, been saved from impact by our helm operator's quick reflexes, but her action sent the *Esperanza* yawing sickeningly, and I felt the gravity ripple as the rotation was briefly interrupted. "Petra?"

"Now!"

I gave a quick nod to Anna, Petra's sister – almost identical, save that her hair was pitch black; a total contrast to Petra's blond. At the helm, Anna hit the hyperdrive controls in response to my cue. A second later, the stars vanished to be replaced by a whirling blue vortex as the ship leapt away.

I sagged back in my chair, sighing with relief. "Good work, Petra," I murmured softly, "like always. You too, Anna."

Petra smiled back wanly. "Now just hope that they can't track us again."

Yes, that *was* the hope.

Clambering to my feet, I walked with her and Anna as we left the cramped bridge and headed to the even smaller general-purpose meeting room off the bridge. Why they'd bothered to add it at all into the original design of the ship was beyond me, but it was too small for any of the general purposes that we tended to have. We could just about wedge ourselves into it, so long as we had no purpose other than sitting still for a drink and a chat after bridge-duty.

Krystyna, our doctor, was already there, and she ran to Anna the moment she came in, grabbing her tightly. Petra and myself exchanged a slight grin, briefly squeezing hands before squaring our shoulders and moving to our places around the table as the others filed in.

I was so damned tired, I just wanted to crawl to our bunk and at least shut my eyes for a few minutes, but I was captain of this ship –

or at least the nearest thing we had to a captain – so it was up to me to do my utmost to get it to some kind of safe haven. Or die trying. I swear to you that I'd damned well *be* dead, before I ever went back to Earth.

"We're in *hyperspace*?" The nasal voice slid up a whole octave on the last word. Meet John Schultz, the most experienced botanist we had on the ship. We'd kept him and two other botanists out of Deep Sleep so they could keep an eye on all the seeds and such that we were bringing with us, but I truly regretted that decision every time he opened his mouth. Hell, I regretted that he'd managed to find a place with the Exodus movement at all. Apart from those three, the doctor and the essential operating crew, every one of the other thousand travellers on the ship was in Deep Sleep in the modified hold.

"Given that we're not all dead or in the process of being boarded, you can safely assume that," I said, fixing him with a level glare.

Whites tend to get intimidated easily when I glare – my size plus the huge *ta moko* on my face have a useful effect on people that way. John was no exception, but he managed to keep the questions coming despite that.

"But how long before they find us again?" he asked.

"They might not," Petra interrupted quickly. "We're jumping for longer and completely randomly. That should shake them."

"But if it doesn't? Our guns are useless – we can't destroy them."

Krystyna sighed. "Why can't they just let us go?" she murmured softly, blue eyes already glimmering.

A rhetorical question, of course – we all knew the answer to that. The powers that ruled Earth and Luna couldn't have anyone fleeing the Sol system – the mega corporations would collapse if they lost their underpaid peons. The world governments and 'moral authorities' feared that people who were free-thinking and who had the courage of their convictions might actually find a haven out there in space. I guess they realised that the descendants of these emigrants, who held such independently diverse views, might come back to Earth one day to bring about a reckoning.

But they couldn't catch us all. Our Exodus involved over thirty ships; the corporate security mob who handled the retention of people in-system had only ten ships at most. The number of security ships with jump-capability was deliberately kept low to prevent crews from mutinying and leaving the system. Problem was, the security men would try their damnedest to get at least a couple of us, so they could tow back some charred hull to hold up on holovision and claim, 'This is what happens to all people who flee the system! Don't do it!'.

"Look on the bright side," I said, smiling, "If they're running *us* down like this, that means most of the others got away. If they'd already shot down any of the others, I doubt they'd be bothering to take such trouble to chase us."

Krystyna and Petra smiled a little in response to my pep talk, but John shook his head.

"That's meant to console us? They won't give up, and even if they do, every planet we've happened across has been airless, waterless, rocky – no chance of survival in such places. We're supposed to be trying to find some kind of new home, but we haven't seen anywhere we can live. There's been nowhere that even has water."

"We'll find somewhere eventually," I said, working to keep my voice level. "We've identified over two dozen potential locations in the Goldilocks zones of stars similar to Sol. One of them must have something that's at least habitable." With all our seeds, stock and saplings we had aboard, plus the thousand of us in cold sleep, we'd be able to make it even in a desert-like world.

"Besides. Recent events have shown us that there are *definitely* life-bearing worlds out there; give us time and we'll find one," Petra added before I got too irritated.

"What if we don't?" John was on a roll now. "I'm sorry, but we may have to come to terms with the possibility that returning to Earth is the better option."

"Returning to Earth?" Krystyna glared at him. "Are you *insane?* We'll end up in prison or dead if we do that."

"Look, just because you're a gay, it doesn't mean that we *all* need to worry about how they'll treat us."

"You came with us," Petra said, a definite edge in her voice. "Even if you're the whitest, straightest man going, *you* left Earth. They'd throw you in the same prison cell as they would any of the more alternative or free-thinking members of the crew."

"But what about that thing we found? We could trade that for a pardon, or for better conditions."

"*No!*" My voice was louder and harsher than I actually meant, but I couldn't help it. "There's *nothing* left for us back on Earth. You *know* that! Almost half the land areas of the planet have been flooded, but only the rich and powerful get to live in the Domed Cities. and they're the only places where life is really safe. My homeland of Aotearoa is totally uninhabitable – it's mostly under the damned sea now, except for the tips of *Kā Tiritiri o te Moana.* Everything that remains is either owned and run by corporations or ultra-conservative lunatics. You know that, why else did you come with us?"

John opened his mouth to speak, but I drove on, "There's no hope on Earth. I'll die before I go back, and most of us feel exactly the same. And I'm *damn* well not turning over the most hopeful thing we've found." Before John could say anything more, I rose. "Now. The ship shouldn't be coming out of the jump for another few hours, so everyone please try to get some sleep."

They began filtering away, but I saw John glowering at me as I headed out. Petra took my hand. "Coming back to the cabin?" she asked softly.

I managed a smile, but shook my head. "Not right now. In a few minutes, yeah. I just wanna see if I can make any more headway at all, y'know?"

She nodded. "But don't stay down there too long, will you – *you* need to sleep too."

I hugged her, gently kissing her forehead, then turned and headed to the nearest hatch. One big disadvantage of flying such a makeshift ship was that there were no elevators on it. A short ladder journey down, then I was at the door of the main medical bay. I walked in and looked across at the room's single occupant.

That occupant looked right back at me now with a beady eye, before hopping over with a light gait and rubbing his head against mine.

I smiled. "Well, you're friendly – we've established that much, if nothing else."

The alien made a loud chirping sound. It wasn't *just* that he was covered in bright, red-blue plumage; his motion, bone structure and song all combined to make it very plain that he was, essentially, a giant bird. He nuzzled me again and I grinned at him, then sat down.

You may think it strange of me to refer to him by the masculine pronouns. At the beginning I'd called him 'it'; but his personality was so strong and so friendly, that it seemed hostile and degrading to call him that. I know that I should have used one of the non-binary pronouns – that's in retrospect really, because what actually happened was that talking to him was so comfortable for me, so familiar – don't think I'm crazy, but he was *so* like my older brother in personality that he became 'he' to me without my realising it was happening. Plus, he had really bright plumage, and that was usually a male thing on Earth birds, so I'd gone with 'he'.

"So. Any hope that you're closer to understanding us yet?" I asked softly. He chirped again and began to preen himself. I sighed. "I guess not, huh?" As he chirped happily, I shook my head. "You don't understand us, we don't understand you. And we definitely don't know what to make of your ship. We've been over it with a fine-tooth comb, and we can't even *begin* to work out the technology."

Petra was the one who had first noticed the weird liquid that the ship appeared to use instead of circuits, but she'd given up in despair when she'd tried to scan it. It was very rare that anything mechanical left my girl at a loss, but this fella's ship had managed it.

I settled back. "Don't worry. Even if I never understand you, I won't go along with that idiot John's suggestion. Not that you know what that idea is, of course, but I won't go along with it. Maybe it's mad, but I feel that there's some kind of cause for optimism just having you here."

I grinned, "Maybe I've been reading too much Emily Dickinson – hope being a thing with feathers and all that – but damn it, you *are* a cause for hope. Whatever else happens, we can take comfort in the fact that we've discovered that humans aren't the only life out there. Even if we've bollixed our own planet, even if we've done everything possible wrong, at least someone else out there got it right, yeah?"

The alien flapped his huge, multi-coloured wings and took flight briefly – not the kind of random flight of the surviving Earth birds, but something that seemed to have definite thought and precision behind it – before landing next to me and nuzzling me again.

"So, you can read my emotions to some degree, I guess. That's good – maybe there's some hope for us being able to communicate after all, huh?"

He sang tunefully, as I chatted away to him, hoping that if I repeated stuff enough times, he might get the hang of what I was talking about. "I don't know what the world you came from is like, man, but it's got to be better than ours. Has to be!" I shook my head. "You ever been anywhere near Earth? Nah, I doubt it. if you did, you'd not want to go back. I mean, you're avian-descended – you and your people must know all about why it's bad to foul your own nest. Let's just say that's not a lesson we've been good at learning," I hung my head, "or much wanted to learn, if we're being honest. "

"As long as some people get to keep living as good as they always have, in domes or in the orbital cities, then the rest of us are happy to toil away in the hope we'll get to be one of the better-off ourselves one day. Even as our air turned poisonous and the water levels rose and drowned whole countries, we just kept on chasing the rat race." I stopped for a minute; to be honest I felt despair – I think you could call it that. The sort of feeling that sits like a heavy weight on your breast bone and makes you feel that it's as much as you can do to crawl out of bed each morning. That's how I felt every day on Earth.

"Well, that's not exactly fair to us workers. When people can't keep themselves fed from day to day, the environment and politics aren't life and death matters; it's as if they've nothing to do with us. Until suddenly they have, of course," I shook my head slowly, feeling the familiar waves of depression rising in my heart, the waves that threatened to wash away any feeling of optimism I was clinging to, like sweeping a drowning man from floating debris.

The alien seemed to recognise my distress, as he nuzzled me again and put a wing over me in a sheltering motion. I smiled at him– a painful smile, but still a smile. "Thanks, mate. You're a good sort, I think, even if I can't understand you." I sighed, "John reckons we should go back to Earth; that it'd be better to do that than get killed out here; better than simply going on and on, never finding a planet where we can settle. I can see why he's scared – *I'm* bloody scared, believe it or not. I brought us all here – the woman I love, her sister, her sister-in-law, all of the thousand who're asleep right now – if I've bollixed up, they'll all die y'know?"

I sighed again. "Maybe it's a Maori thing! We fought against the *Pakeha* when they invaded our islands, even though they had guns and we didn't. We fought to try to save Aotearoa, even when we could see it was going to be claimed by the waves. When we became a scattered people, we fought harder than ever to keep our culture and traditions alive, even as people tried to grind us down."

My face bore testament to that – it had been my father who made sure I got the *ta moko.* As the bird nuzzled me again, I squared my shoulders. "But as long as we're alive, as long as we're still flying, there's at least a chance we might find some kind of haven where we can settle. And I'd rather die chasing that chance than go back to a world where there's no chance at all."

"So would I."

I jumped, then shook my head as I saw Petra waiting at the door. "Thought I told you to go to bed."

"You did. I ignored you," she grinned. "It always feels empty without you."

I fought a grin of my own as I stood up. "What? A single metal bunk bed feels empty without me in it? Hmm. Either you're going mad, or you got it bad for me."

"Maybe both." Still smiling, she took my hand. "I have faith. Faith that we'll get away, faith that we'll find somewhere to set up a home, to have children who can breathe clean air and can be whoever and whatever they're born to be."

Somehow, when she talked to me, I felt all the doubt wash away. Well, most of it anyway. Enough that I could summon a genuine smile and squeeze her hand back as she led me from the room.

"*Ahika? Ahika!*"

I jolted awake in the narrow bed at Anna's voice, loud in my ears.

"Uhhh...*what?*" I demanded, blinking my eyes as Petra stirred behind me.

"We just came out of hyperspace. There are planets! We've identified four so far."

I was sitting up instantly, Petra already scrabbling for her glasses and me for a shirt.

"On my way. Keep an eye out for any sign of pursuit, but I'm on my way."

I dragged on my trousers, uttering a muffled swear-word as I whacked my elbow against the edge of the tiny bedside table. Then we were making our way to the bridge; clambering swiftly up the ladders, me silently cursing the necessity that had left these ships without stairways, let alone lifts.

After what seemed an eternity, we were falling through the bridge bulkhead. Anna looked up from her instruments, gesturing animatedly towards the main screen.

"Look! I launched a probe. It's reporting an atmosphere!"

I looked. Sure enough, there it was. Lower oxygen content than Earth, and it looked a bit more arid, but the probe was showing a breathable atmosphere and surface water.

I grinned from ear to ear. "We can make this work. Bring us in closer; we'll take another look. But keep an eye out – we don't want to be caught unawares."

Anna nodded, working the helm controls as the planet swam closer and closer. As she worked, Krystyna hastened onto the bridge, followed by John.

"Is it true? We've finally found somewhere?"

"Early to say," I cautioned. "We'll need to survey it from orbit first, then examine it on the ground."

Krystyna nodded hastily, reddening a bit. "Of course. We'll need to make sure there aren't pathogens that're harmful to humans; make sure our crops can grow there *and* don't all get gobbled up by the soil."

"Make sure there aren't any horrible predators that bleed acid," Anna cut in.

I mock-glared at her. "No, it wasn't the *Predators* who bled acid," I joked. A weak one, but it got us all laughing in relief.

Well. Almost all. John was frowning at the panel. "It's not going to be easy," he said eventually.

I shook my head, smiling. "Nah, mate. It's going to be a lot of hard work and sweat. But just think! It'll be on a planet where we're not coughing our lungs up from the pollution; we won't be worried about flooding either."

"There's oceans and riverways, too.' Petra looked up from her own scanners, a look of childlike wonder on her face now. "We could actually swim, or see fish."

I took her hand gently, nodding. Petra had grown up near flooded Hamburg. She'd always told me that it wasn't the flooding itself that she minded. It was seeing just how grey and lifeless the sea was; a soup of human runoff and effluvia, no vitality to it at all. The idea of being able to see an ocean that was the same as the seas used to be on Earth was amazing. We'd only seen that in footage from the past. I could imagine how excited she was – she wasn't the only one. I was already making plans, maybe the old vids have instructions on how to build sailboats. Maybe *I'd* do that – like the Maori of the past who first sailed to Aotearoa.

If the planet would let us live there, of course. I had to prepare myself for disappointment. But *if* it did.

John sighed, "Well, if we've made it, then I suppose we should get on with things, right?"

"Hey, be happy man," I advised. "We might have done it, you won't have to worry about the law scooping you up."

As though some perverse god or spirit had heard me, it was at that exact moment that the alert klaxon blared again.

Anna's eyes widened. "*Scheiße* – they're back!"

I felt like groaning, but instead I stood up, moving over to a free terminal. The weapons terminal. "Right then. We're not running again, not unless we have to. Our weapons have been totally ineffective so far, but we have to find some way to stop them – I'm not leaving now we've found somewhere we can maybe call home."

"We should surrender!" John burst out. "Plead for mercy or something."

Petra turned to me. "They're signalling."

OK, that was new. "Let's hear them," I said, straightening in my chair even as I checked that the autocannon were loaded.

There was a pause, then a crackling cold voice came over the speakers. "This is Security Vessel *Order and Peace* to fugitive spacecraft. You are ordered to stand down immediately and return with us to the Sol System. Non-compliance will result in your immediate annihilation. " I took a deep breath. "This is Ahika

Herangi, commanding the *Esperanza*. We're not about to return anywhere with you, I'm afraid. We have civilians in cryo-sleep, including children – would you really destroy them?"

"Stand down immediately and return with us to the Sol System, or you *will* be destroyed." The voice didn't waver at all.

I bit my lip. I hadn't wanted to do this, but needs must.

"We took quite a few rare and precious artworks with us when we left Earth, including jewelry and gold. We were hoping to have them for future generations, to show what we'd left behind. But we'd be happy to turn them over to you, if it meant you turning a blind eye."

That could work – the ships were primarily run by corporate thugs, many of them were the kind who'd happily ignore orders to enrich themselves.

There was a brief pause, before the voice came back again. "Many captains might've taken that deal," it said coldly, "but not me. I'm not about to let you people have your own new, clean planet, while me and mine are stuck with Earth. Who do you think you are, that you should be the ones to spread humanity? People like *you*?"

I gritted my teeth. *Fucking crabs in buckets.* "You realise you've already failed? Eight ships followed us from Sol. Even if each one gets a target, that still leaves a lot of ships spreading themselves out over deep space. Unless Earth's going to send you out again and again to hunt down colonies, they're gone. Even if they do that – the galaxy's a big place, how're you going to find them all? Why bother?"

"We'll try, damn it. We'll try. You have one minute to reconsider. This is your final warning."

The signal cut off. I took a long, deep breath. "Anna, get ready to move us away. There's an asteroid belt in this system, we can use it to…"

"You're going to try to fight them?" John demanded, eyes wild.

It wasn't me who answered this time, it was Petra, "If you think we're running back into space after we've found somewhere, you must be mad. We take them out – nobody else knows where we are, we'll be safe."

"No! No, this is insane! I'd never have dreamt of coming with you people if I hadn't lost my business! But if you think I'm risking my life for this quixotic madness..." He stopped shouting for a second, then had the gall to say, "If you really want them to leave us alone, offer them that useless alien and its ship! They'll reconsider then."

"*Or* they'll take it and then murder us all," Anna cut in.

"At least we'd have some chance…"

"We're not giving a living being over to them," I spoke firmly. "Do you really imagine that I'm going to hand that ship to them? Give those people who run Earth the kind of technology that might let them find all the other Exodus ships, that might be better able to track down dissidents? Not one chance in hell!"

"So instead you're going to risk all our lives on this madness," John's eyes were wild now, and his voice had a ragged edge to it, "on the slim chance that we might be able to destroy that ship?"

"We can do it, if we all work together. The cannon haven't done much, but if we're smart, and we use the asteroid belt..." I began.

I broke off, as the door hissed open and two men stalked in. I recognised one from engineering, and the other as one of John's botany colleagues. My eyes narrowed as I realised that the first carried a crowbar, while the other was holding... *Oh no.* It was from the equipment lockers – an explosive device for driving soil-sample spikes down through rock. Discharged into a human body, it would obliterate it.

"What's this about?" I demanded.

"This is myself and my friends here thinking that your utopian dream is *not* worth dying for," John growled. "When we thought that you might actually get us away from Earth, we were willing to try. But we're not going to fight. No, we're going to contact them, and offer them the alien in exchange for a full pardon."

He smiled shakily. "Maybe they'll even give us space in one of the orbitals for that kind of service! I'd say they will. No need to go back to Earth, or try to turn a damned wilderness into somewhere livable."

"You'd be happy to do that, yeah," I asked, "live in a nicely managed little satellite paradise, while people down on Earth die from pollution and hunger?"

"Think *you're* any better? You just wanted somewhere comfortable to live. You couldn't wait to get away and leave Earth behind."

"I didn't *want* to do that. This isn't about *my* goddamned comfort – it's about giving *some* humans a place where they can live free, be themselves, and maybe have a shot at surviving beyond the day when Earth can't cope anymore with all the abuse that humans have given it." I met his gaze. "It wasn't ever about me – at least mostly it definitely wasn't. It was about humans having a damned *future*."

John gritted his teeth. "We don't have time to debate this. Get out of that chair, and..."

His hand began to move for his belt – I guessed he had some kind of concealed weapon tucked into it. I didn't give him the chance to prove that. My left hand shot out, grabbed his belt and yanked him straight onto my rising fist. I shot into a standing position, as I yanked the suddenly-limp botanist in front of me, keeping him between me and the guy with the spiker. His eyes widened. He hesitated, still aiming the spiker but keeping his finger away from the thumb stud, while his friend hefted the crowbar.

Both of them focused on me, weighing up their next step.

The shot rang out, deafening all of us on the bridge. The man with the spiker went down, a bullet-wound blossoming on his upper shoulder. Petra stepped forward, holding the handgun that'd been hidden on the bridge.

"Drop it," she said sternly, aiming steadily at the guy with the crowbar. "I react poorly to people who threaten my partner."

I grinned at her. "Thanks, sweetheart."

Anna and Krystyna stepped forward to restrain the mutineers and administer first aid to the man Petra'd shot. As they did this, John came to his senses.

"What happened?" he gasped, his hand to his forehead.

"You and your pals brought tools to a gunfight," I said bluntly. "Bad mistake. Don't worry, though. If we live through the next few minutes, I'll make sure you get a fair trial."

He spat, "You bastard! You'd see us all die for a bloody pipe dream?"

"No."

I was already working the targeting computer as Anna, returning to the helm, pulled the ship around and accelerated towards the asteroid belt.

"But I'd happily lay down my own life for hope. Back on Earth? There's no hope for the future, no prospect of things getting better. All anyone on Earth is doing is just waiting for the end, so stuffed with propaganda that they think everything's going to be just fine; or propping up a failing system in the hope that they'll be able to make it through."

I shook my head. "I'll never support any of the corporate or religious lunatics who run the world, and I'm not going to try to hoard my life when there's damn-all to live for. On another planet where we can start over, at least there's hope. And I'd happily die for a world where the people down below here now, our children, and our grandchildren can have hope for the future."

Even as I spoke, I could see the pursuit ship firing up its engines, coming right at us. I triggered the autocannon, sending a hail of solid projectiles right at it. Even from here, I could see that they were just bouncing off the thick armour, but I had to try.

"Ahika!" Petra's voice was urgent. "The cargo bay, it's opening!" She turned towards me. "it's the alien – his ship's flying out!"

My heart jolted in my chest. "What? More mutineers?"

"I don't know... It's coming around now."

I looked at my screen. Sure enough, it was looping effortlessly around our ship and heading straight for the pursuing Earth vessel, faster and more smoothly than any human ship ever could have done. I took a breath, ready to say...

I have no memory at all of what it was that I was going to say, because it was right then right then that it happened.

The energy beam fired from the alien ship was something that our computers couldn't even register – the sensors tried to analyse it, but the system crashed. There was a rush to reboot it. They managed that in time for us to witness the enemy ship hanging, dead in space, entirely deprived of power.

I turned to the others, "Jeez, am I really seeing this?"

Petra nodded, a shell-shocked look on her lovely face, "We all are."

"There's a signal coming in," Anna cut across our general stupefaction. "I don't recognise the frequency, but it appears to be coming from our friend's ship."

There was a low whirr and the main computer monitor lit up. In place of the usual read-out of the system, was the beaky face of our erstwhile alien guest. He trilled once, but then the speakers on the bridge played out English words.

"Are you alright, my friends?" the alien asked softly.

I swallowed before I was able to speak, "`We surely are, thanks to you." My eyes widened as I realised what was happening. "*Hang* on! You understood us all the time?"

"I could. I did want to tell you, but I had to be sure."

I shared a glance with the others, then Petra asked, "Be sure about *what*?"

"You." The alien fluffed his feathers slightly, then continued speaking. "You were quite right – our people *did* visit your world. Not openly, of course, nor even visiting the surface. We watched from orbit, monitoring your signals."

I winced, "You must certainly have been disgusted, seeing how humans behave to each other and to our planet."

"Not really," the alien trilled. He preened briefly before continuing, "The fact is that, in the past, we weren't much better than you. We almost destroyed our world – not through pollution and environmental destruction as happened to Earth, but through what you would call a nuclear war. Over two-thirds of our entire population died. It was thanks to the ingenuity of a small number of our ancestors and the hard work of all the survivors, that we came through it and were able to reach for the stars."

He fixed us with beady eyes. "It was because of the parallels we saw between ourselves and you humans, that some of us were sent to monitor Exodus. Not just to monitor but also to help you elude the ships that pursued you. Unfortunately, my ship was damaged, so I was unable to help you. But when I realised that *you* were helping *me*, that you had rescued a being you'd never seen before and whom you had every reason to fear, I thought it might be an opportunity to learn more about you. I wanted to discover if your fears would get the better of you, or whether – with nothing more than the slimmest of hopes – you would strive for your future, despite everything arrayed against you."

I looked at the others mind racing, as I finally realised that thanks to this alien we were finally *free*. I searched for words, but they kept slipping out of my head.

In the end, it was Petra who spoke out, talking as she crossed the bridge and took my hand. "People shouldn't be blamed for being afraid, or for not being able to summon up the courage to try for dangerous change," she said. "But for many of us – like my man here, even if he's suddenly on the tongue-tied side – a life without hope isn't a life at all. And you need to fight for your hope sometimes, even when the chances are slim."

"Agreed," the alien said emphatically. "It is in that spirit that I offer you a further possibility. This world *is* one where you could safely settle. It is, however, a little too close to your homeworld for certain safety from discovery and attack. It is also somewhat stark. I can bring you to a world that is far more suitable for settlement; one more like your homeworld but with no sentient species; one where you could truly thrive in safety. Will you follow me? Bearing in mind that you know nothing of me, and bearing in mind that not all races out there are like mine. Some are more primitive, some more aggressive, and a few are truly terrifying.

He looked around at us all, gazing intently at each of us in turn. Then he asked, "Are you willing to continue the path you've started?"

The others looked to me. I nodded, "Absolutely."

The alien trilled again. "I hoped that you would be."

His ship swung around and, as Anna worked the helm controls

setting us on a course to follow our good fortune, Petra put her hand into mine.

MEET THE AUTHORS

Cameron Armstrong is a writery guy from Canada who likes movies, video games, strategy games, reading, cats, his wife and kid, and thinking real hard about the Human Condition. He wonders if you, the person taking the time to actually read this little blurb, are reading it simply because you're curious about who wrote that one story you liked, or if because you're wondering how these writery people go about doing their writery business. Like, do they even have jobs? Aren't they cripplingly depressed over how dismal their chances are of reaching a wider audience than their parents and immediate circle of friends? He would answer yes to most of those things, but the trick is write for yourself first, not other people. That way, no matter how many rejection letters you get or how many of your half-finished novels get shuttered away into the Dead Forever folder on your PC's hard drive, you'll have created something worthwhile; a little artifact that you can leave behind for the world to say, 'I was here, and I had ideas, and I wrote some of them down'. Who knows? Historians of the future may comb through the vast data reserves of the 21st century's long-fallen Internet giants, brush it off (digitally speaking) and give it a read. It worked for H.P. Lovecraft.

Paul Carroll is a writer and comic creator from Dublin. His work primarily focuses on the extraordinary, be that through magic, science or just downright chaotic. He is a founding member of both Limit Break Comics and Cupán Fae. His obsessions include tea, foxes and spreadsheets.

paulcarrollwriter.com

Quinn Clancy is a writer and programmer from Dublin. Fascinated by fantasy at a small age, she has consumed everything passed down from her equally fantastic minded family. She started her writing journey in school when spelling was difficult. Spelling remains a mystery, but the stories in her head have only multiplied and now she just wants to share them with you all.

Kat Dodd is an American transplant that escaped from a small town in Arkansas right between Toad Suck, Pickles Gap, and Wooster. The first story they ever wrote was in a purple crayon in their journal, and Kat hasn't stopped writing since. Their typical genres are a conglomeration of fantasy/sci-fi, LGBTQI+, and YA, with a thread of romance going through them. Kat lives with their Spouse-Type-Creature, though Kat frequently forgets to feed him.

thekatdodd.wordpress.com

Axel Kelly got bitten by the writing bug very early in life, though he'd like to think his writing has improved since he started. He also got bitten by the sci-fi and fantasy bugs early in life too, thanks to his family. Originally from West Cork, he now lives in Dublin, working for the Civil Service. He had a number of short stories published in anthologies during his time in college, and since then he's published a number of stories in Cupan Fae's anthologies. As well as enjoying writing for its own sake, it's let him get to know some really great people, especially in Cupán Fae. He is massively grateful to his family, for all their support and kind proofreading since he began writing, and Helen, Paul and Kat, for giving him the opportunity to share his work with a wider audience.

ABOUT THE GROUP

Cupán Fae is the caffeine-filled home away from home for fantasy writers in Dublin.

Established in 2015, Cupán Fae meets weekly to discuss current projects, create writing prompts, collaborate on new ideas, workshop problematic plots and provide psychological support for characters with three minds of their own and a battle axe to grind. We also dive into the looking glass of popular culture and deviate into discussions about politics, the world of literature, and anything else that can help us put off writing during those moments when a WIP is more like a WHIP.

Printed in Great Britain
by Amazon

18539128R00092